THE SKY HIGH ROAD

Also by Moses L. Howard:

The Human Mandolin
The Ostrich Chase

Writing as Musa Nagenda:

Dogs of Fear: A Story of Modern Africa
The Ostrich Egg Shell Canteen

THE
SKY HIGH
ROAD

Moses L. Howard

Jugum Press

Copyright © 2015 by Moses L. Howard

First print edition: May 2015
ISBN-13:978-1-939423-30-6
ISBN-10:1939423309

Library of Congress Control Number: 2015943107
Jugum Press, Seattle, Washington USA

Cover by Lisa Tilton Design
Book design by Annie Pearson

Published by Jugum Press
505 Broadway East #237
Seattle, Washington
Find ebook editions at www.jugumpress.com
Contact: JugumPress@outlook.com

For Missoura Bradley Howard

Whose loving quote was:
"Can anything good come out of Nazareth?"
— John 1:46

THE SKY HIGH ROAD

ONE

JASON'S FATHER IS DEAD AND his mother lay dying of AIDS in the back room. His grandmother had come all the way from her home at Nanansi to take care of Mama. Now she was scheming to send him and his sister Katura away.

Jason would never say "No" to Grandma. He'd never say to her that he wouldn't do something she asked. That would be disrespectful. He didn't say he wouldn't go. He didn't say anything. He kept quiet and went outside to tend the goats and check the fence.

His family was a zoo observed by the park animals, or so it seemed. The animals watched Jason's family through the ten-foot-tall metal fence with two strands of barbed wire running along its top next to the big game park. Hartebeest, aggressive warthogs, huge elephants, and colorful zebras were all familiar visitors to the silver fence managed by his father.

Jason's father was a decorated park ranger. With one shot he felled a buffalo that charged a Land Rover full of tourists, mostly women and children. He had captured members of a band of poachers who raided the Uganda Queen Elizabeth National Park and hunted white rhinos almost to extinction, killing them for their horns.

Before the fence, the animals had wandered over the family property; sleek brown antelopes ate his mother's garden vegetables; elephants left piles of steaming dung on the path in front of their house and trampled the lawn. Goats got lost to leopards while Jason attended school.

He knew it was dangerous to go into the game park. Although when his father was alive he had warned Jason, when Father was away Jason had climbed over the fence to get a soccer ball kicked there, and he'd hiked in the park if the animal herds drifted away. Confident he could always climb back over speedily without the animals seeing him, he'd often visited the park. He'd practiced moving in and out like his father.

Now was a good time to do it again, to escape Grandma's demands. No buffalo or warthog or rhino was visible. None of the big cats like lions, or cheetahs lived here. He could outrun any other animal. Wearing tennis shoes, he would be fast like one time when his father had caught him. Daddy swatted him with a tree branch. *"Jason, you better listen. Animals can smell you before you can see them."*

Jason had smooth brown skin and short curly hair. He was listed on his soccer roster at Budo School as five feet eleven inches tall. He was muscular with strong arms and legs. He leaped up, caught the top strand of the fence, muscled up, and twisting, flipped his body over, and landed on springing feet in the park. Over the fence, twenty yards ahead, he scanned down the hill to the tourist station, the lake, and the parking lot. No animals around, so he went to the edge of the flat park and looked through the low trees and tall grasses. A group of tourists were walking with a ranger toward the lake. Others stood on the verandah, gazing after them. Everything looked normal in the park. Suddenly, he became aware of movement behind him.

2

When he whirled around there were two giraffes nibbling on high tree branches. Oops! They weren't there the last time he looked. Instinctively, shivers ran up the back of his neck. How could he have been so mistaken?

He turned abruptly and headed back. Several monkeys in the distance cavorted in the bush and low trees between him and the fence, and a little farther down, a water buffalo coming up the hill. He wanted to run, but he knew better. He grabbed the highest barbed-wire strand, muscled up, and flipped himself into the yard. Relieved and ashamed, he heard Daddy's warning again in his head. *"Jason, animals can smell you before you see them."*

Then he went around to the front of the house to watch the park rangers—dressed in their green uniforms and yellow hard hats like Daddy used to wear—unload long bare eucalyptus logs to put up the long-awaited electricity light posts near the baobab trees.

He'd come outside just to get away from Grandma's talk. After checking the fence and the goats and wandering danger- ously into the park, he crept back inside the spacious living room.

Grandma was straining, looking over her eyeglasses to see the labels on the new medicine bottles that the AIDS nurses brought for Mama. The nurses visited with medicine and advice at least once a week. Grandma grumbled that she could hardly see in the bright daylight, and her difficulties at night were worse. Her choices for lighting were a smoky lantern, a torch, or candles. She straightened up and looked at him intently. "Please, go to my house and bring back the solar lamp."

When Grandma gained that lamp, she had lost her son. Daddy had bought this special lamp for her when he went to a conference for rangers in Nairobi. She bragged that this lamp needed no oil. You set it out in the bright sun and its strips soaked up light and stored it. At night it just glowed. It was a solar lamp.

"If we bring your lamp here, what will you use when you go back home?" He said that just to delay her. He was just reaching for any excuse he could get.

Katura, his fourteen-year-old sister, was in the bedroom off the hallway making beds. Grandma rarely allowed the children into the back room where their dangerously ill mother rested. Although the visiting nurses said that AIDS could only be spread by sexual intercourse and the blood and other liquids from sick patients, she was very cautious.

Jason couldn't say how he felt to see Mama lying there; sometimes she barely breathed. She had lost a lot of weight and never called out or laughed or even told him and Katura to do chores or homework. His heart thumped; he lowered his head and looked away every time he glimpsed her. Daddy was already dead of it, and now Mama might go the same way.

Jason knew Grandma wasn't mad at him; she wanted to convince him. That was her way. He knew she loved both him and Katura. They visited her at Nanansi last year, and it was the happiest time they had ever had. Even though he loved Grandpa and especially his jokes and the funny things he did with them, Jason wasn't aiming on leaving his grandmother all alone here to take care of Mama and Asia, their baby sister. What if Mama died or something while he was gone? It would be like he'd abandoned her.

Grandma wasn't angry when she looked straight at him, but he knew right away it wasn't the long-suffering "ask me anything" grandmother that they were used to. Although she had the sweetest smiles and looks most of the time, she didn't have them this time. She was all serious, like she had been thinking all the time. She had been up nights for the two weeks she'd been here to take care of Mama.

"What do you mean, Jason? What will I use when I go back? We'll cross that puddle when it rains. And it's not even rainy season. Do you think I have only one lamp at home? I have the old one and a beautiful one that your grandpa bought for me years ago on a trip to Kampala, long before Katura there was born." She pointed to his baby sister with the hand that held the plastic medicine containers. "Asia wasn't even thought of back then." She paused. "But the very best one is the solar lamp."

"Daddy bought us a lamp, too, and lots of nice things from a *duka* in Mbarara." Katura said wistfully from the bedroom door.

"Your daddy did a lot of things . . . good things. He did . . . bad things, too. He didn't take care of himself or his family." She averted her half-closed eyes and twisted her mouth firmly to one side as if she was avoiding taking an unpleasant medicine. She looked more intently at the medicine bottles. Jason knew by her looks and pauses this was unpleasant for her; yet, it was something she had to talk about. "AIDS kills people . . . more people die from hiding the truth. They cannot or will not see." She repeated this every day.

By her action he could tell it was a painful subject; her sweet familiar face soured with frowns and grimaces, and her eyes looked at you and through you. She must be thinking about her only son now dead and her responsibility to take care of his wife and children. She reminded them again that by his careless actions their father had killed himself.

Katura and Jason heard from the nurses who brought the medicine about prevention and the danger of contracting AIDS. Now that Grandma had started in on the topic, the whole painful thing was coming out again, because she insisted on going over everything to keep their minds focused on their safety.

Her words hurt Jason. "I would love to see Grandpa, but can't I wait and go there with you?"

"I won't be leaving here for some time. I can't leave your mother. I have lost my son. I won't go through that again. Don't you remember your father? Is he already dead and gone in your minds?" Over the tops of the medicine bottles, she stared at them. "Katura, don't you remember him? . . . How he loved you and took you everywhere in the park? You rode up on his shoulders, frolicking and seeing everything below you. Don't you both remember his wide, prideful grin, his green uniform and yellow park ranger hat? What about his courage when he ran the poachers out of the park? They returned and stole everything while the family was away. They even stole lamps and tablecloths off of the table."

Then she paused and turned away, folding her apron and wiping away tears. "Your father was about to get electricity here, but the main lines were so far away. It is taking longer than anyone thought. But now I need a good lamp to read medicine bottles to save your mother's life."

"I could go to the stores and get a small lamp with a wick, and we could just wait awhile. You shouldn't be here alone, just you and Katura."

"You and Katura will go to Grandpa to get my solar lamp while I stay and look after your mother and the baby," Grandmother said in a firm voice.

He looked at his grandmother then as if she had gone crazy.

When Katura heard her name, she came out of the bedroom and stared, too. "No, Grandma! That can't happen," she blurted out.

Her words made Katura and Jason rebel. "No, Grandma! It is not nearly right. I know you want what is best, but I am kind of the man here."

"Yes," she said quickly, "but if your father is an example, we have seen what a man who does not know can do as a leader. That's why I want both you and Katura to learn to see the dangers and to gain the knowledge to fight them."

"Now, Grandma, you can't do everything by yourself. You're trying to do it. But it won't work."

Katura spoke up. "Grandma, do you know what you are saying? We just couldn't leave you alone *no how*."

They stood firmly against her. This time they would disobey.

TWO

THE BABY BEGAN WHIMPERING, THEN *Whaaah* crying, and there were a few loud grunts and moans from Mama in the back room. Jason wondered if they had heard the arguing with Grandma and wanted to be a part of it. That's when Grandma put aside the medicine bottles and jolly-like said, "Wait until I see to my patients. I'll take care of you in a little while."

While she was gone, Katura and Jason faced each other, shaking their heads and planning how they would attack her plan and refuse to obey her for her own good. They were a family. If Grandpa were here, Jason thought, Grandpa would side with them. They simply would not go away and leave her alone with the danger from the animals and from the poachers returning to steal what remained of the property of his father, their enemy.

Jason noticed that Katura was wild-eyed and frightened. Right then she looked older than he had thought of her before. Her more grownup appearance was probably what scared Grandma. Infected men without morals might be tempted to choose her as a victim. Many believed a sexual encounter with a young girl could cure the disease.

For the first time Jason realized that she was a beautiful girl, with her hair woven in a fine basket-weave pattern by Grandma. Her dresses and blouses showed her budding breasts. She always wore necklaces of colored beads that Daddy had bought her. Her skin was smooth; her black eyes sparkled. She was excited and defiant, a lovely sister. He was proud to go to school with her, but he didn't want to travel alone with her, walking on roads or riding buses. He didn't know if they could protect themselves from outside dangers. He wanted her safe at home.

"I don't know what Grandma means that we should go together to Grandpa's. That would leave her here to take care of Mama and the baby and the entire little farm," Katura reflected. "We can't do it."

"I know! It's too dangerous and there's too much to do. Grandma is old and she couldn't manage it."

"I don't see that. Grandma can manage lots of things when she can see them. Grandma is a trained nurse. She's been to the best schools. Don't forget she breaks rules when she thinks they are wrong. Remember when she was a girl and they didn't like girls riding bicycles or girls wearing pants? She was among the women of her time who did those things anyway." They laughed at the things Grandma had done. She had been Nora Kajubi, one of those "Gayaza Girls," so named by Jane Tops, the famous feminist British headmistress at the high school.

But they were determined not to let her do this. They didn't understand her reasons for sending them away to see things. "She's right about us not having a lamp, but I won't go away and leave her here alone," said Jason, determined.

They listened to Grandma talking softly to Mama while crooning to the baby. The baby had quieted down, her soft crying melded into playful contentment. Jason tiptoed quietly back to where she coaxed and fed spoons full of medicine to his mother. Mama was more like her child, instead of her daughter-in-law. As she held and soothed Mama, propped up in her arms, Grandma was the strongest person he knew.

They sat on the couch, waiting for her to return. He glanced through the glass window to the park and caught a glimpse of the slow fluid movement of a giraffe, feeding near their fence. "Katura, do you remember *our* giraffe?"

She grinned. "Yes, it was *ours* when Daddy was alive." The fence was not set up and the herd of zebra came every day, too. But one morning this beautiful long-necked mother giraffe and her baby showed up. "She stretched her neck and ate leaves of the plum trees outside our garden. They were not afraid but shy, turning their heads, cropping tree branches. They looked at us like they wanted to be near us, like friends."

It had been a long time since they'd talked about *their giraffe*. Jason had not thought of it since they talked about it at school when he was in upper Primary and Katura was in lower. The teacher had asked about where and when students had meetings or experiences with animals. Some students boasted about trips to the zoo at Entebbe or seeing the monkeys in the rain forest near there. Some students said animals came to their farms at night and they chased them away. Others saw animals at the movies or more often on the television after they were filmed for audiences in Europe and America. Katura and Jason were the only students who lived near animals and had experiences with them almost daily.

They proudly told about their life on the edge of the national game park where they had personal hyenas, warthogs, elephants, and buffaloes. The animals observed them; they were inside of the fence, a zoo of humans. It was fun to talk about it then, as it was now to relive it, while waiting for Grandma.

When she returned, her eyes were sparkling. "Ignorance is a great evil. Living here near the park you children have missed seeing and learning important things that could save your lives. A trip away from here will enlighten you. That's another reason I need you to go for my lamp. In order to make the right choice, you must see everything clearly. Without my solar lamp, I cannot easily see the right medicine for your mother. You can't see much because you have lived your life here in darkness with the animals." She shook her head, for she recognized their rebellion. "After this journey, you will see and understand more about the dangers in the world."

Jason shook his head, refusing to agree to leave her.

Katura, folding her arms, said in a new firm voice, "Mama taught me to cook and to take care of the baby. And now I will take over those responsibilities."

He knew that Grandma was impressed, for she paused and looked tenderly at Katura. At Gayaza she had been taught several languages: English, Kiswahili and other vernaculars such as Luganda, Kinyarwanda, and Runyankore. Her practical nurse license and many years of medical work had sharpened her understanding of suffering and care. She listened to world news to have a clear and current vision. She was proud of her educated grandchildren.

She brought out a box from the closet with surprising old things. The first was Jason's little transistor radio he had used to listen to news and music while tending the goats. She also placed on the table Daddy's radio and cell phone, uncharged with only a few minutes left on it, and his work computer. The park administration had copied the evidence against the poachers.

Jason's transistor radio with new batteries sputtered with static yet was loud and clear enough to hear the BBC. She smiled and gestured to shush them, her voice excited. "They're announcing a breakthrough program of funding by Bill and Melinda Gates, the Microsoft billionaires in America. They are attacking AIDS and malaria through a foundation headed by Bill Clinton, the former president of America." They listened to the announcement.

"We are not alone with this epidemic. It is a worldwide fight."

Jason thought about his school friend, Biraro, and their dreams of their future professions. He had just taken the Senior-4 O-level examinations. Now he was waiting for the results so he could pursue studies to become a bona fide herbalist.

"You kids don't know, but when Clinton was president of the United States, Hillary Clinton, and her young daughter Chelsea visited our Women's Advance Group in Murchison Falls. Your father was then a trainee for park ranger. I was there. Hillary Clinton spoke to us. After her visit our group raised money and built a clinic near my house. They are helping us. And today, we must help ourselves."

Grandma said that they must go because these people were giving money to buy medicines. "We must do our part. We have to participate."

Her words touched a deep belief inside Jason. That's why she said she had to see and read the labels and they had to keep up-to-date with everything. She needed Jason and Katura to use the cell phone and keep in touch with her on their trip to Grandpa. She said there must be another cell phone around the house. She began searching in cabinets and drawers.

Soon she located another on the floor in Daddy's closet among some boots and goggles, but neither phone was active.

They were not charged and had only a few minutes on them. Minutes or talking times would have to be bought. All family cell phones must be charged.

"I know you kids want to help. You can help more by going to Grandpa and bringing me the lamp so I can read the medicine bottles that President Clinton and Bill Gates are sending us, and maybe we can save your mother and your little sister. I won't be alone. I can get someone nearby to help out."

Jason and Katura couldn't say anything; their resistance was gone.

"Kids, don't you worry. Nurses visit often and I will hire some neighbor boys to look after things and help me around the house and take care of the goats."

Jason used the few minutes left on the phone to call Biraro, who promised to come and help Grandma. He lived nearby down the road past the secondary school across the lake. Then Jason and Katura planned for the next day when they would begin their journey to get Grandma's solar lamp.

THREE

THE NEXT MORNING, BEFORE LEAVING, Jason swallowed his malaria pills.

"Katura, take your medicine now. Grandma, make her."

"Grandma, Jason wants to be my boss. I know how to take medicine. I will take it later with the water bottle in my backpack."

Grandma looked at her sternly and went back in the room to take care of the baby. "See that you take it every day," she said over her shoulder. Katura ran to catch up to Jason, who was already down the road.

Jason thought it was just like any school morning except he would have left Katura at the girls' school while he went on to the boys' Senior school across the lake. Today they were walking along with a crowd of women, men, and children. Jason passed Logan's house, catching a glimpse of him feeding goats in his backyard.

Katura waved to her friend Chala and then to Auma who lived with an old uncle and aunt on a coffee farm. Jason knew that Katura felt sad because Chala's mother and father had died of "malaria" in Mubende, although everybody knew it was really AIDS that had killed them. People felt it was a disgrace to say a family member died of AIDS. Grandma was different; she believed that as long as it was a secret people did not see the danger. At first Jason and Katura were ashamed at school when the news got around about their father and mother having the "big A"—AIDS—but many people were dying of AIDS. Many families kept it secret until it came out when their loved ones died. Or they still hid behind the mask of "malaria." Others stated the facts. More people owned it now; people realized it was wiser to see and name the danger.

Jason had come around to Grandma's way of thinking about being honest about diseases. But he noticed that Katura still worried about what people thought of her. Other students, who knew about their father's death and their mother's illness with AIDS, moved away or did not play games with them at recess.

Jason and Katura knew that AIDS passed from person to person by fluids like contaminated blood. And that most often it was passed during sex. It was not like the Boda Boda, the little motorcycle passing them now. It was made in Dubai and could be bought and transferred from person to person in all of Africa. AIDS was not like that. Katura knew it, but Jason noticed she was quick to say about AIDS, to some girl or boy, "But we don't have it, we don't have AIDS. We have been tested. Jason and I are clean of it." She would point her finger to her chest and twist her wrist pointing a thumb at Jason.

"You don't have to do that, Katura," he said. "Accept it and know what you know. You can always share what you know about diseases and medicine, but you don't have to give a testament of your health. People will find out the way they want to, when they need to know." And he added, "But we can stay healthy and safe from malaria with the medicine and by avoiding mosquitoes."

At school Jason and his friend, Biraro talked about illnesses and how to avoid them. Biraro always said, "No matter where you are, you have got to guard against mosquitoes putting that tiny parasite in you while they feed on your blood. Mosquitoes do not take holidays. People should not relax but be vigilant."

Jason and Katura continued past the schools with silent yards and closed windows, lonely places without the loud play and laughter of children. He wished schools were open year-round.

Motorbikes and bicycles threw up little circles of dust around them, and the motors *chaurrred* and *pika-picka-pikaed*. The morning dust had absorbed the night dew and would not be free flying until the sun beamed down and dried it.

The air of the morning was heavily scented with fruity fragrances from nearby farms, gardens, and small orchards. Jason and Katura breathed deeply and trudged on beside the people. When they had passed the schools and few shops, the people on the road thinned out. Only a few workers crossed on the ferry to where the main road led to the towns north in the direction of Grandpa's place.

At the lake they walked out on the high log wharf and stood with the coins for their fares in their hands. Along the shore, up and down, the lake fishermen in small boats shook out nets, readying them for the day's fishing. They sat smoking in log-hewn canoes. In the water, there were a few shop-fitted, well-made boats with motors. Most people crossing the lake went by ferry, which was less expensive than hiring a private boat.

The steel-keeled ferry had a ballast of logs tied to its side. It took a lot of time crossing the lake, but it was safe except for the one time that hundreds of people tried to cross at once. The ferry, overloaded, tilted and sank in the middle of the lake and many people died.

Grandma pointed to that as a case of poor vision or ignorance. It was broad daylight but everyone had business over on the other side at the same time. No one could see that it was more prudent to wait. Everybody's desire blotted out the danger, like Father in a dark room trying for what he wanted.

On the ferry Jason and Katura found the ferryboat not crowded. Well-spaced seats were anchored to the side with many ropes. Jason sat on a high twisted coil of yellow sisal rope, and Katura sat in a chair near the edge of the ferry. When the ferry started up and the water whirled and churned around the sides of the ferry, she leaned way over and let her hand trail in the water. The water was muddied with silt, so she could not see deep into it.

"Little woman," said one of the boat workers, "Not safe to put your hands there. A crocodile might take it and pull you in the lake." Jason turned toward her, laughing. Katura shrugged; the workman was only trying to frighten her. He went on about his business of loosening and tightening ropes along the keel but soon returned to stand by Katura.

He had a hand-sized river perch on a string tied through its mouth and gills. He stood beside the girl and flipped the fish into the water, holding on to the string tightly. Instantly, a bracket-roughened green crocodile head rose up, clamped on the fish, and yanked the line out of the ferryman's hand. Katura's hand flew up to her throat. She gasped, her eyes wide in shock.

"Woo! Jason, I could have lost my arm."

"Yes," he said, "sometimes we cannot see the danger that is near. There was no light down in the water to warn you." He sounded as if he were quoting his grandmother. The ferryman had not gone away. He stood by Jason, who sat on the thick rough coils of twisted yellow sisal ropes. "Not for sittin' . . . danger," he said, pointing to the thick yellow rope coils. "Please sit in the chairs."

Jason dismissed him playfully. "Oh, I'm a footballer. I like it rough." He threw his muscular chest up, "I don't need a chair." Jason took a shrinking, oval kiwifruit from his pocket, squeezed it several times, threw it in the air and kicked it upward with his foot as it fell, and kept it in the air with follow-up kicks, rhythmically as he did at soccer practice. He was very agile and controlled, turning himself and kicking, kicking the little ball-like fruit.

The ferryman stood eyeing him, "Do you know what the ends of rope are tethered to?"

Jason paused in his play, puzzled. He tossed the kiwi in the air several times and, turning quickly, caught it. He shook his head; he did not know what the ends were attached to. He could not see the ends and had not thought of them. He only knew how comfortable the seat on the top of the twisted coil was.

The workman shook the end of the rope that was tied around stanchions in the side of the hull of the ferry. "This," he said, "is good for you." Then he moved farther down to the side of the ferry and shook the end of the rope attached to the heavy metal anchor. "This, the other end, is tied here. In deep water, four men throw this anchor overboard to stop the boat. The rope uncoils quickly because of the anchor weight. It zips into the water. You would be pulled with it and would become crocodile food. You, tough footballer, like it?" He looked for an instant at the startled Jason and moved away down the ferry's length to other duties.

Katura, wide-eyed, glared at Jason. "This boat isn't safe!"

After that they walked up and down the center of the ferry-boat. Jason kept his eyes on the approaching landing where people were waiting. He hoped to see Biraro waiting for the ferry when it landed on the other side of the lake. He should be there to cross over to help Grandma. He'd envy Jason's opportunity to visit with the herbalist, Mr. Kasamba, Grandpa's friend and neighbor whose shop was located in the little town of Nanansi near the Shelsia Clinic, named after Chelsea Clinton. It was the clinic Grandma had helped to start.

Both boys were interested in local herbs and medicine. They wanted to study diseases and medicines, not to be doctors but to make people well by finding new local medicines. Most strong effective medicines were made in England, France, America, or other foreign countries.

Their chemistry teacher, Mr. Eru, had told the class, "We have medicine right here in Africa. The problem is the research has not been done to standardize the dosages and purify the medicine. Our doctors and herbalists are called 'witch doctors' by the foreign press because they don't have degrees or Western training. Since there is no standard here, everyone has to get medicine from abroad like the Boda Boda from Dubai and like the solar panels from China to power the cell phones."

Jason and Biraro and some fellow students now aimed to change the belief that everything used here was made somewhere else. They wanted things made right here in Uganda. They planned after their O-level results to take any scholarships and study anywhere in the world, but they would resist the temptation to be bought by riches. They would not remain outside of their country to make money, but instead they would study, gain the necessary knowledge in pharmacy and chemistry research, and then return to their country. They would set up research stations like the ones at the Fishery Department on Entebbe Road or the internationally known Viral Institute at Entebbe.

When they were in Senior-2, they had visited the Viral Institute with their schools on a two-day trip. Both boys had resisted their parents urging them to be doctors or businessmen. They did not know how they would manage to get the education and money to complete their dreams.

They knew people like Dr. Kaseka, who had gone to America as a young man and became a doctor. He was much in demand there. He remained there for twenty-five years, making money for his family. He was acclaimed in America, but that did nothing for Uganda, which had given him his basic foundation in education. Yes, he took care of his family, but how did that help Uganda?

Had Dr. Kaseka and others like him returned with their knowledge, many people might not have died of AIDS and malaria. When Jason learned this, from that moment he knew what he wanted to do. At that time, Jason's father, the park ranger, was sick with AIDS and died the year before Dr. Kaseka returned.

In preparation for their future, Jason and Biraro read everything on mosquitoes and how they bred and how malarial medicine worked. They were interested in where the medicines came from and how they were made. It was not that simple to find information about AIDS. No cure had been found. They were also disappointed that they had so much trouble finding how medicines were made. They searched their school libraries, but much of the information they hoped to find was not in their books.

There were a few computers in school and the boys looked up individual medicines on the Internet discovering some were extracted from plants and others were *synthesized*. That was a new word, meaning made from, or put together from, different sources. Jason and Biraro grabbed onto any new word, found the meaning, and made it theirs at once. They had to study widely and quickly to make sure they knew enough to go ahead and discover medicines. There were many more diseases—Ebola, malaria, kwashiorkor and jiggers, and others newly discovered—and not enough medicines to treat them.

Medicine men were around them in every village, but there was no one to ask about medicine and no pamphlets on how medicine was made. Someone in the village sold medicine for almost any illness, but none could or would tell you about the medicine. Most people were afraid to ask, because they thought their illnesses were the result of some enemy practicing magic on them or their family. Medicine men usually guarded their knowledge as secrets and only passed it down to some chosen relative.

The two friends were both forwards on the same Senior soccer team. Biraro was short and stocky with a wide-faced grin and bulging muscles; he had the best ball control of any boy on the team. Jason was lightning fast, lean, and lanky and could dodge and flow wherever the ball was. He confused opponents. The boys had devised signals, yells, stops and turns, misdirections, and one-word directions. To head a ball left, one would call, "Side door right or left"; the other would hear the signal, knowing that the caller had detected a weakness in the opponent's game and would immediately position himself to follow up or receive the ball.

Now Jason and Katura stood in the center of the ferry watching the workmen. The eddying of the blue lake water became muddy from debris as they approached the bank. They watched people standing there waiting to cross in the opposite direction. Jason scanned the crowd waiting to board.

He looked for his friend's face. He was disappointed and worried when Biraro did not appear.

FOUR

JASON REMINDED KATURA, SINCE THEY had little money, they should walk in the daylight but always stop somewhere before dark. They should ride the bus when they could afford it. Jason hesitated and looked down the main highway.

"What are you looking for? What's the matter?" Katura asked.

Jason shook his head. "Don't you think it's strange that Biraro was not at the ferry on his way to help Grandma? I am worried now. He is usually so dependable."

"Maybe he overslept. School is out. He will probably catch the next one."

Jason shook his head. "I don't know . . . we can't just go on not knowing. No, I think something is wrong. He is never late for school. We may have to go back and wait a day. Grandma needs help."

"Let's go up the hill. Maybe someone has seen him or has news."

The chugging ferry, already loaded with cars and scooters, started back across the lake. Jason and Katura walked up the tarmac roadway to Mbuzi, a small hilly town noted for goats. They saw many types of goats, bearded and clean-chinned, horned and hornless, mixed colors and solid brown, little kids and old nannies. Billies and does grazed in the back of shops, others were tethered in pens, and a chorus of goats' "Naas!" filled the air.

In several shops they saw slaughtered goats hanging upside down from metal hooks, their severed heads dangling on racks. Customers ordered the meat. Butchers sliced and wrapped slabs, heads, feet, and other parts into banana leaves and then placed the wrapped orders in the shopping baskets of the women and servant cooks.

Jason thought he recognized a woman. He led Katura through the crowd closer to get a better view. After several women moved aside, he saw her clearly. Yes, it was Biraro's mother. He recognized her colorful dress and the bangles on her long arms. Why was she here instead of their cook? He moved closer. People crowded around the butcher. Mrs. Ochingo must certainly know about Biraro's promise to help.

"Hi, Mrs. Ochingo. Is Biraro? . . ."

She didn't seem to hear him. There was a lot of chatter from customers demanding service, and loud motor vehicles close to the curb made it difficult to hear. He wanted to be polite, greet, and wait, but she seemed distracted. And she didn't notice anything around her. She impatiently bargained with the attentively nodding butcher.

"My husband is very disturbed today. Something terrible has happened at home." She paused, shook her head. "He's sensitive to the types of goat meat." She flung her bangle-adorned brown arms out. "He only likes the flavor of the Angora goats. That's why I had to ride a taxi all the way up here to buy meat for stew."

"Yes, it is very good," said the butcher. "That's why I am charging you more per pound for it."

"But how do I know you are telling the truth. My husband will be able to tell right away if it's Angora. The last time . . ."

"You can't tell once the skin is taken off. Trust me, it is pure Angora. We killed and dressed it just last evening. It is one and a half shillings per pound. How many pounds for you?"

"It must be Angora."

Jason walked nearer. "Hello, Mrs. Ochingo. Is Biraro still at home? We are very happy that he's coming to help Grandmother." She turned from the butcher, at the same time pushing her basket nearer to where he was slicing the goat's thigh.

"Oh, Katura! Jason, I saw you coming uphill, but I am peeved with this butcher. Oh yes, I must tell you right now, we are very upset at what Biraro has done."

"He promised Grandma that he would come to help her today. Katura and I are going to Grandpa, and I can't leave her alone. I am hoping to see him in two weeks when we meet to discuss our O-level results. I have been studying medical terms and hope he has been studying also. We are . . ."

Mrs. Ochingo was vigorously shaking her head, a puzzled look on her face. "I am very sorry, Jason, but our house is in turmoil. I know he promised to help your grandmother, but you will not believe what our son has done. My husband is very grumpy because Biraro has left home. I'm afraid unless something is done, he won't even be around to see his O-level scores. We are all very upset at home.

"I would have sent the cook or my daughter for this meat, but the cook is missing since last night. His family is worried. I fear that the army must have him. They might also have taken Mbabazi, our daughter, if I had sent her here."

With a decisive flourish, the butcher cut the meat and wrapped it in banana leaves, smearing the green leaves red with a bit of goat's blood, "Two pounds!" He put it in Mrs. Ochingo's basket.

Then Mrs. Ochingo said, "On second thought, I must see the skin from that goat whose meat you sold me. I must be able to tell my husband for sure when he argues about flavor, that it came from an Angora goat. He is very sensitive to taste. He can tell."

"Well, he should have his own goats," the butcher said angrily.

"Still, I know he can be wrong, but he did used to tell me Biraro could not be trusted. I didn't believe him until today when we woke and found him gone."

The butcher grumbled, but he went back into the shop to search for the goat's skin.

Jason was beside himself with questions. He whispered to Katura. "That's a big letdown. What can Grandma do if he doesn't help her? We'll just have to go back."

Katura shook her head like she did not want to return home. She stared at Mrs. Ochingo, who watched the door until the butcher returned with a bucket. It had the white goatskin and some offal covered in flies. He held it up with a large wooden spoon and stirred the buzzing flies away.

"You see, now, it was Angora!"

On the nearby road, cars, bicycles, and scooters screeched and busily proceeded among the shops set close to each other down the narrow highway. A bent and battered brown van badly in need of washing pulled to the curb on the opposite side of the road. It stopped near the cell phone-charging kiosk. It reminded Jason to charge his cell. He watched a tall man get out and try unsuccessfully to open the door. The man had a military posture, wore a blue suit and a red fez.

Mrs. Ochingo looked convinced and satisfied with her purchase of the goat's meat. "All right, I can now tell him for sure the meat is from an Angora goat." Then she turned again to Jason and Katura. "We hope you get good O-level results and keep on with your studies. Don't you let anything get in your way."

"Yes . . . but Biraro promised our grandmother that he'd come and help her while we are away. He is a level-headed fellow and I can't think what has happened," Jason said. He was puzzled; he couldn't believe Biraro had just run away. "Where did he go?"

"Our daughter saw him leave. He talked to someone at the door and closed the door. He came back briefly to whisper instructions to Mbabazi, said he didn't have time to tell her details, said to tell us not to worry. You know he is a religious boy, and now he has gone off with a group of religious soldiers. Our daughter says he's joining the army. He said to her hurriedly before he closed the door against her, over his shoulder, he'd be all right. He told her they needed young soldiers, boys and girls. Then he quickly closed the door." She stared nervously at both of them. "So you two are off to your Grandpa, leaving your Grandma there alone with your sick mother and her child." Mrs. Ochingo sounded distracted.

Jason looked all around. "We can't leave her alone. We must return home."

"But she sent us to get her lamp," said Katura.

Mrs. Ochingo paused. Suddenly her eyes brightened "I know, instead of Biraro, I'll send Mbabazi to help her." She seemed to breathe a sigh of relief. "I couldn't bring myself to go to church after I found out our Biraro had run away. A church was to blame."

Jason and Katura exchanged glances. "How was a church to blame for Biraro running away?" Jason asked. "What did the church do? I thought you said he'd joined the army."

"Well, it is that church army that he's run away to."

"Church army?" said Jason.

"Yes, you must have heard of it. It calls itself the Christian Liberation Army and it intends to bring down the government."

The butcher who had been listening behind his counter, his knife poised over a slab of goat, suddenly said, "Oh, God help us! You mean the LLA. That's what it calls itself. The Lord's Liberation Army."

"Are they here? Then Allah protect us," said another customer with a white beard. He folded his hands together in front of his face and bowed. "They're a bad lot!"

"They come at night, attacking villages," said a woman with her head tied in a colorful scarf. "They magically appear when you never expect anyone and disappear when they have done their mischief."

"I thought they caught their leader, a man called General Kony or Corknee, or some such name," said the butcher.

"No, he escaped right out of the shackles!" said the blue-suited cigarette buyer standing nearby, listening.

"They sometimes take over whole towns, beating and killing those they can't convert or convince to join them, and then flee before the government army can arrive," said the butcher.

"The government should protect us. I have lost a good son," said Mrs. Ochingo.

"They thrive on youth. They grab young children who follow orders without blinking their eyes," the woman with the colorful scarf said. "It's a shame what they do with children, arm them and order them to shoot anyone. They must obey to get food and stay in the good graces of their ruthless leaders. I have heard of beatings and bites."

"The government should protect us," Mrs. Ochingo repeated.

"But the government can't be everywhere," said the butcher. "How can you protect every citizen from a large band of thieves roaming the entire country, disguised most of the time, and murdering and raping people in the name of God? How do you protect people against such a horde? They're worse than a scourge of locusts when the fields are ready for harvest. They swoop down and leave not a young human standing."

"Yes," Jason said, "I, too, have heard of them. It doesn't sound like something Biraro would join."

"Join? They may ask, but in the end they force children to join. They give them a gun," said the butcher.

"I've heard some sad and terrible stories about the mistreatment of children in their camps," said another customer with a long face, paying for a package of biscuits.

"I am going to my church and pray, and everyone should do the same," said the man in the red fez. Agitated, he returned to the parked van where the young driver gunned the motor and sped down the road past the sign for the bus stop.

The butcher watched them go. "Yes, prayer is good, but even though I pray to Allah, I keep a sharp knife near."

"Do they take girls, too?" Katura asked, fear in her voice.

"No army can exist without girls and women. Yes, my daughter, you are in danger, too."

Now Jason realized they must return home. He also feared for his sister's safety traveling with him on the long journey. "Katura and I must go back to help Grandma since Biraro can't help her."

"I could lend her a good lamp and maybe you wouldn't need to go back." Mrs. Ochingo offered. Jason hesitated; their grandmother had her mind set on them going for her own lamp.

"Mbabazi is older than Biraro. She could help your grandmother while you are away. She would be safer at your house. I could accompany her down to the ferry this very evening. She is at home waiting for her nursing course to start. It would be good practice for her."

"But the goats . . ." Jason protested.

Mrs. Ochingo chuckled, "Mbabazi can manage. She does everything for our family."

She had convinced the children to continue their journey although Jason was still worried about Biraro. They crossed the road to board the next bus. He glanced at the kiosk, touching the cell phone in his backpack.

Mrs. Ochingo, on the other side of the road, waited for a taxi to take her home in the opposite direction. After she got in a crowded taxi, she waved to them.

FIVE

THE CROWDED BUS CRUNCHED TO a stop. The long-faced man who had bought the cigarettes and spoken heatedly about the Liberation Army got on first. Jason and Katura paid their coin fares of half a shilling and followed him as he found a seat near the middle of the bus. Katura and Jason stood in the aisle with several other children. The children were scrubbed and dressed in their Sunday best with hair combed and bright colorful tennis shoes. They talked of Sunday school and several of them recited Bible verses. "Remember the Sabbath and keep it holy." "Blessed are the pure in heart. The Lord is my shepherd and I shall not want." "The Lord has given us light." They sang the verses from different quarters of the bus. "God is great!"

About the middle of the bus sat a Moslem family, the father wearing a robe, the son in a dark suit, and the mother dressed with her head and shoulders covered by a beautiful white shawl, only her eyes visible. Four big boys, rough Senior-2 types, sat in a row on each side of the bus.

Three girls and four boys soon got off at the youth center sign. The Moslem family got off at a small hamlet where a mosque stood back from the road. Five children, chanting verses and slapping each other merrily on the shoulders with laughter, ran through the bus door at the same time. Jason and Katura moved to seats near the front of the bus. Katura sat inside and Jason sat near the aisle.

A few miles farther along, the man with the long face nodded to Jason and Katura and left the bus at the Sunrise Missionary Church sign, an arrow pointing into a banana field. When he left, the bus was half full, with quite a number of boys and girls Jason's and Katura's age going to church services at a nearby seminary. The bus was almost emptied at the Covenant of Good Hope.

The driver pulled up to a lone adult figure standing with a short stocky boy beside an isolated building with few trees. The young man immediately boarded the bus, pushed by the stocky kid, and told the driver, "Wait! They are coming . . ."

Then Jason saw a group of men and boys dressed in green uniforms and berets rush toward the bus from where they had been concealed among the thick banana trees. They all carried guns, and two of the boys carried big long rifles. The ones carrying the guns pointed in front of them pushed onto the bus, boys and girls shoving guns in front of them. They were forced, urged, and pushed on by bigger boys in back of them near the entrance.

The thin boy of about fifteen had his arm in a sling. Fresh wounds with patches of blood streaked his face. His head was covered with a blue bandana on one side and a beret pulled down over the other. Jason recognized his friend's voice and was about to call out, "Biraro!" when this boy's eyes lit up as he looked at Jason and rushed past him down the aisle, pushing against him, passing him close with his hand to the side of his lips. "Situation dangerous, Jason. You don't know me," he whispered as he passed. "Very important! Danger. Be quiet. *Shee* . . ."

Katura whispered, "Jason, that's your friend. Biraro!"

Jason shushed her, whispering, "Katura, There's danger! Something's scary! Wrong! You saw his injuries. He said it's dangerous to recognize him. Just wait . . ."

She answered loudly again, her eyes large, frightened. "Jason, look at those boys with guns. I'm scared."

The rush of young soldiers onto the bus was followed by a tall green-uniformed man with a red sash over his shoulder, and a light green beret. He carried a heavy wooden, beaded walking stick. Jason thought he had seen this man a short time before, dressed differently, back riding in a beat-up van in Mbuzi town. Now he wore a big gun in a holster on his side. He eyed the group. Jason knew he led them by his stern manner and the tilt of his shoulders, eyes alert, watching as he herded the group in front of him and immediately took control of the bus. He shouted in the face of the driver, standing over him, waving the stick like a scepter.

"Don't stop anywhere along the way. Take us to Slingo! We have our own transport there."

The driver pushed backward, trying to rise up from his seat, looking around to protest.

"What do you mean?" The tall man did not hesitate; he used the stick as a club, banging it down hard several times on the driver's skull. Jason almost felt the blows, wincing with each strike. "You must listen!"

Ugh! Bam!

The stick came down. "When I repeat!"

Bam!

"I hit like this." He struck downward with the stick several times rapidly on the driver's head and shoulders. Jason saw a gash and blood oozing out of the side of the driver's skull. "Your job is to drive. If you can't do that, I will replace you,"

The driver looked up with frightened eyes, shivering and cringing at the tall intruder. He fumbled with the gearshift and put the bus in motion. Jason caught Katura's hand and headed toward the door, but the rough hands of boys holding guns blocked the aisle nearby, and another grimacing boy with a long knife pushed him roughly back into his seat.

"Nobody moves from this bus. You are all now in the Lord's Army. You're all soldiers. I am the recruiter, and I get a special bonus for anyone I recruit who is in Senior school. We need officers. I am the commander," said the tall man, who looked all around with a crazed half smile.

Jason at once pushed forward, resisting, struggling, and protesting, but two big boys grabbed him. Together several of them lifted him off his feet, and pushed and shoved him back down roughly every time he tried to move. Over the shoulder of his assailants, he met the eyes of Biraro, whose lips signaled the words, "Sit and wait." At his side, Katura started crying.

"Jason, how can we be soldiers?"

Other children whimpered and fretted. Alarmed, they called for parents. "I'm going to Sunday school," one protested.

The man with the stick yelled to his followers over his shoulders. "Watch me. Report!" Jason could not tell to whom he was talking.

"Keep the damn children quiet." He swiveled his head around several times with a menacing stare. "I can't concentrate." That's when Biraro moved back and forth among the children, shushing them and saying, "Don't want any one hurt," showing his bleeding ear. "Everything is going to be nice, just wait and see."

It looked to Jason as if Biraro was looking for a way to escape but found the front aisle blocked. Jason looked back at the back seats where there were fewer children. When Biraro passed him, Jason mimicked action they used during soccer matches. He pointed with a bobbing, twisted neck and head and yelled out, "Side door, blocked, try back!" and quickly pointed his head in that direction. He smiled when he saw Biraro go down the aisle toward the back again.

There were two adults on the bus: a sleeping old man and a very short woman with a basket in her lap and a blanket. Jason had seen her buying goat's meat in the market. Jason saw the sleeping man had been wide awake until these last people got on. Now he slumped down and literally snored.

With the bus moving, the commander finally paid more attention to his captives. He turned and stood up, hovering over everyone, and spoke loudly to all of the children on the bus. His voice boomed out a hot, friendly wind.

"Who wants to be soldiers in the Lord's army? Raise your hand and Uncle Munonga, the commander, will love and take care of you, and when we get to Slingo everyone gets a gun. We have guns, many of them! And you get to own one, no matter how young you are. Don't wait until you're grown up. You can shoot now."

Jason was glad that only those already carrying weapons raised their hands. The others were frightened, crying. Not a child except those already armed raised a hand to be a soldier; Biraro slumped down in his seat across the aisle from a short muscular boy. Biraro pretended to sleep, but Jason saw him furtively glancing around; Jason knew by this behavior the regular Biraro who acted this way in a game of soccer. He was planning something. Yes, he was quietly planning something.

Biraro was on a seat by himself near the back door, but there was a little boy sitting on the seat opposite him.

The leader called back over his shoulder to some unidentified person. "Do your job! Tempo! Tempo! I know you are watching me. Keep your eyes on me all the time." Jason looked around trying to follow the commander's eyes to identify Tempo, but the commander was looking about the bus, not settling on anyone. He reminded someone named Tempo to somehow guard the whole bus, but especially to watch him for signals.

At first Jason thought Tempo was a name given Biraro, but he never responded. No one answered. The little old woman looked out the window while boys were running their hands up and down their guns, joking and pointing them.

The commander looked in the rearview mirror over the driver's head or over his shoulder—he had to watch the road, watch the driver, and pay attention to what went on in the bus. Everyone stared at him. Jason felt Katura shiver against him. He reached out and grasped her arm to reassure her, but he was at a loss of what to do. Where was the bus headed?

"You, there on that middle seat . . . five back." He counted as he bobbed his head. "Come up here, boy." He pointed a crooked finger at Jason, over his right hand holding the stick.

Jason turned his head aside as though he did not understand. But Biraro stood up and pointed sharply to him and motioned him to go on up. Jason reluctantly left Katura and went up the aisle. When he stood beside him, the commander started quizzing him: "You, boy, do you go to school?"

Jason glanced at the driver's bleeding head, then looked all around, thinking what he should do. The commander hefted the stick, drawing back his arm, ready to strike. "Do you go to school?"

Jason raised his arm. "I did, sir."

"Well, you don't need to go to school any longer! You can be an officer right away. Now! How would you like it to be in my army?"

Jason didn't answer. He looked at the driver's bleeding head again. He tried to glance back at Biraro and Katura. Now the two big boys with guns stood immediately behind him.

"Listen! Pay attention, boy! What grade were you?"

"Senior-4, sir."

"Another Senior-4. We have one with us already." He pointed in the rearview mirror to where Biraro sat. "Do you know him?"

Biraro quickly signaled Jason to shake his head.

"No, sir," Jason lied.

"Well, you can be a lieutenant right away in charge of all guns. Don't make me scar you. You are promoted the day you enter. I need Senior-4 boys to train for officers. How long before you're promoted in school?" Jason did not answer. "What is your name, soldier?"

"Jason, sir." He glanced at Katura slumping down in her seat.

"Then you're Lieutenant Jason, an officer in God's Liberation Army. And you're in charge of all guns. Don't you like that?"

"I don't shoot, sir."

"Well, by the Lord's army, you will shoot plenty. Have you ever held a gun?" He pointed to the guns held by the boys behind Jason.

Jason remembered his father's guns propped in the corner of his closet back home. He almost told about his father's guns. But he glanced back at Katura who made a weird frowning face at him with large frightened eyes. "My grandmother sent me. Please let me go. My mother is dying."

"Speak up. What is she dying of?"

"I don't like to say it to everyone, sir."

"If she's dying, boy, she's dying. Everyone will know soon anyways. Is that your sister with you?"

"Yes, sir, Mother is dying." Jason felt this answer confused the commander.

"Well, it is too bad. But you, both of you, are in the Lord's Army now. I am keeping you as soldiers."

"But, sir, our mother . . ."

"She'll die any damn way. Can't you see that? What are you whining about? Die this, die that!"

"But our mother will die, sir, if we don't come back . . ."

"Go sit down and send the girl, your sister, up here. Up here, now! She is prettier than you."

The bus driver drove at a terrific speed. Jason lurched slowly back to his seat, touching Katura. "Say 'Sir' a lot. Don't say things to make him angry. He's crazy!" he whispered.

"What are you telling her? Stop talking and send her on up here. Now!"

Katura swayed up the aisle of the speeding bus. The guns held by the swaying boys in the aisle clacked as they bumped together. The driver passed a stop with people waiting and waving at him to stop but the bus sped on. Katura stood in the aisle by the commander.

"You aren't afraid of me, are you?"

"Noooo, sir," she said, her voice shaking. "I am a good obedient girl to my grandmother. She sent me, sir."

"You want to be in my army and do whatever I say, don't you?"

"I can cook and I can bring water and help, yes." Katura bubbled out a series of answers.

"You want to be in my army, don't you? 'She sent me, sir.'" He mimicked the girl. "Who is this grandmother anyway?"

"Oh, you'd like her, sir. She makes good fried chicken and cassava cakes and baked yams, sir. She's a nice grandmother, sir, but our mother is dying, sir, could you—"

"Quiet. No, I can't let you go. If I did let everyone go, I'd never have an army. Now just keep quiet. What is your mother dying of?"

"Oh, I forgot," she put her hand quickly over mouth. "Oh, Grandma told me to take medicine every day. May I now please take my medicine? Please, sir, let me go."

His attention was drawn to three big boys arguing, wrestling over a gun, pointing it at one another, whirling it about the bus with everyone ducking when it pointed toward them. "Tempo, can't you see what's going on. I told you, damn it, to watch!" The boys sat and soon the commander pulled Katura toward him and whispered something that Jason, half out of his seat, strained to hear.

Katura slapped about her ear as if she was fanning away a noxious insect. Jason started up from his seat, but noticing that Katura was handling her interview well, he sat back down.

"My grandmother sent me, sir," she said again. "Let me go, sir."

"No. I can't let anybody go. You're all soldiers from now on."

"All of us?" She waved her right hand in a circle, taking a chance to look back at Jason and Biraro and the others. Jason knew she saw her backpack on the seat and must have remembered how she had refused to take her malarial medicine that morning. "Yes, sir, everyone at my home is sick. Can I take my medicine so I won't die?"

"Medicine? You don't look sick. What are you sick of?"

"My grandmother told us to take it. My medicine is in my backpack."

He pushed her away with one hand. "Bring me your back-pack and your brother's, too." One hand shot out and grabbed the flesh of her right arm between three fingers. He closed and twisted his fingers on her upper arm. Katura winced, almost doubling her body and yelling in pain.

Jason got up and started for the front. The man held up the hand that held the stick to stop him. The boys with guns blocked his movement.

"Girl, go and sit down." Katura was crying and holding her arm as she ran away down the aisle and flung herself down beside Jason. The man's hand waved menacingly in the air. "Bring those backpacks now."

Jason looked around and picked up the backpacks. He remembered what Biraro said. But he wanted to fight, to challenge this man with the stick. He saw that the bus driver's head still bled. He glanced back at Biraro. His friend's head was down, his eyes averted, as though he waited for something. Jason took the backpacks to the big man standing over the driver, his stick poised threateningly over the driver. He struck the driver on the shoulder and head. Blood drained down his face covering his eyes. The bus went speeding past waiting passengers, never stopping.

Jason saw the driver slumping and moving erratically in his seat. His hand moved off of the steering wheel to his face; his head was bled more profusely. Blood ran down across his face. The commander jabbed him with the wooden staff.

"Watch it!" He grabbed the steering wheel and yanked it to this side and that. He hit him again and again on the head and on the face with the staff. "You won't join up with the Lord's army, eh? You are damned and might as well be dead." Furious, he turned to look toward Jason and the others. "You, back there, take heed. This is the discipline of the Lord's Liberation Army. This is nothing compared to what you'll see meted out to disbelievers when Chief Commander Kony gets here. When he's around, everyone jumps when he speaks."

The driver kept wiping his face. When he turned his head to look at his tormentor, Jason saw blood running down into his eyes. The driver had difficulty keeping the bus straight on the road. A few cars passed, meeting it, and the bus was going fast and swerving across the road.

"Everybody call me, Munonga. It means Mister Big." The man kept looking out the window for his turnoff, Jason thought, where he was camped and would meet other soldiers in his army.

Munonga suddenly hit the driver's shoulder and ordered him to stop the bus. "You, big boy, Senior-4. Biraro, did you say?" He pointed over his shoulder. "Take this wreck of a driver to the back. I'll drive this bus myself. Watch what I do, Tempo. Always watch me!"

Biraro came up past Jason, touched him on the shoulder, and whispered, "Patience," as he glanced toward the front. Jason whispered a soccer call to him, for when they saw the chance to score: "Side blocked, use the back." And then Biraro helped the driver toward the back of the bus while Katura moved closer beside Jason.

The commander now in the driver's seat gunned the motor a couple of times and headed the bus down the road at a fast speed. The muscular little boy who had been sitting with Biraro but now sat just in front of Jason and Katura jumped up and ran up the aisle to the commander and shouted, "Stop! Stop now!"

Munonga was going too fast, and by the time he turned his body around and looked back, the back emergency door flew open and both the driver and Biraro jumped from the moving bus. Looking back through the open wind-flapped door, Jason saw them rolling, picking themselves up, and getting off the roadway. With difficulty they ran, hobbling into the weeds along the roadside. The driver, leaning on Biraro, was badly hurt.

The commander braked hard. The fast-moving bus skidded across the road leaving a rubber-smeared line in the black tarmac, nearly hitting several oncoming cars. But the bus had gone too far from where they had lost the two passengers for him to go out and catch them. He shook his head as though it was too much of a problem for him to manage the bus and runaways at the same time. The short boy started to leave the bus through the front door but the commander shouted to stop him. "We'll send someone to chase them up. Get them later." He drove on. "Watch me. Watch everything."

"That kid must be Tempo," said Jason.

Katura looked all around, scared and excited. "Jason, that friend of yours, Biraro, is smart. He escaped. What do we do now? That little boy has a gun."

"Wait for our chance to escape. Be quiet," he whispered. "That little one with the gun doesn't act like a kid. He is too grown up for his size." They watched the "little kid" move up and down the aisle looking into every face. When he stopped at their seat, Jason saw long clan marks on the side of his head and face. And then he saw his eyes. They did not have the bright sparkle of youth; the lashes lay wrinkled and crumbled, an amber sediment lay settled in the center near the nose bridge. His eyes were old. He was a man in a kid-sized body. Jason looked at the well-developed, strong muscles in the arms and the firm set of the lips and strong jaw. As he watched, the "kid with the gun" snarled once at a child, revealing old teeth, discolored as if he smoked cigarettes.

Jason patted Katura's shoulder and whispered to her, "Be careful of that one." He nodded in the "kid's" direction. "He is a small grown man, probably the commander's body guard."

"Body guard? But he's so short and small!"

"He may be one of those small people from the Ituri Forest in the Congo. He's already grown up. You see, he is the only one with a handgun. He's the one the commander speaks to when he says 'Watch me!' It's probably a familiar order."

"But he's a little kid, a child."

"No, look closely at his hands. Gnarled fists with old scars. The nails are discolored and broken from manual work."

Katura breathed heavily with the knowledge and fear of it. "Is he the only old one?" She looked at the other young children from ten to fourteen years old. "He's an old man in a child's body. He's horrible!"

The old man, "Kid" as Katura called him, moved back and forth up and down the bus aisle with keen eyes, head swiveling with each detected sound. He paused, animal-like, listening.

"Don't stare at him, Katura. I think he's the only one we have to fear. Don't draw his attention."

He stood by their seat now, looking intently at them. "They talk much. I don't understand." He announced with his head turned toward the front, speaking to the commander.

The commander answered over his shoulder, "Never mind. In camp, we fix them. Watch everything now."

The little man-child walked up and down the aisle. He closed the flapping backdoor through which Biraro and the driver had escaped. Jason was watching for the chance for him and Katura to jump through it. He ached for action. The front door was blocked by big boys. What kept Jason in his seat was his sister. He would have dared anything, but he had the safety of two of them to consider. So he waited.

Six

THE COMMANDER BROUGHT THE BUS to a crunching halt alongside a large banana plantation on the outskirts of a forest. He stood and extracted a Bible from his briefcase. Opening it, he put his hands among the pages instead of on it. He flipped pages as if he searched for a passage. He glanced about the bus at his prisoners, raised his free hand, and swore them into his army.

"You are all recruited into the Lord's Liberation Army. This is our temporary camp." He nodded his head in the direction of the forest. "We will soon occupy offices in the capital at Kampala in the parliament building. Be proud you began the journey to there, here in the bush."

The commander sounded like he was rehearsing a speech he had heard Kony make or that he intended to make to a larger crowd in the future. After glancing at a paper that fluttered in the page of the Bible, he repeated the speech.

"This is the camp of the Lord's Liberation Army. Soon we will own the country and the big offices in the large capital city of Kampala with the parliament buildings all ours. But that starts here in the bush." Then, with his hand still in the Bible, he said again, "I declare you all in the army. Now, everyone follow Tempo."

Tempo, standing in the bus's door, pointed with his hand-gun to a path that led through the banana fields into the woods. And the little Pygmy strutted off of the bus, holding his hand-gun up in front of himself and looking all around as if he sought a dissenter to shoot. Everyone filed off the bus except the old man, who still crouched in his seat feigning sleep. Eyes closed, he leaned, face buried in his bag. He refused to leave the bus. Jason was held tightly in line by big-armed boys on either side.

Some boys and girls yelled in protest that they were going to Sunday school. The old man still refused to move. Tempo stepped back in the bus, stood in the aisle near the old man, raised the handgun, and shot several time at the roof of the bus. The loud sound of the blasts of bullets tore at the metal roof of the steel bus making a terrible, loud, reverberating, crashing sound. The children held their hands over their ears. The old sleeping man leapt up, came spryly off, and headed the line up the pathway off the road into the waving banana trees.

While they were thus averted, Jason snatched up Katura's arm like a relay runner and propelled her alongside of him, their feet clattering in a mad dash around the bus. They weaved forty yards, a good ways down the road, jumping out in front of passing cars, leaping up and down in the middle of the road, diverting honking car horns, and trying to hail a taxi.

The commander and several boys chased after them and caught them as they dodged back and forth near a Land Rover whose driver almost stopped for them, but the commander shouted to the driver of the Land Rover to go on.

"Go on! Go on! I am their father! Go on!" And he grabbed Jason in a strong grip. The big boys came to hold his arms, and several caught Katura and brought both of them back, struggling.

The commander hit Jason several crushing blows with the beaded stick while some boys held onto his arms and legs, but the hits didn't land solidly because Jason kept dodging and bringing his shoulders up to catch the force of the blows. It was difficult to hold Jason and hit him. He kept moving and dodging at the same time. Jason kept yelling encouragement to his sister.

"Fight, Katura! Kick and scream! We have to fight. Remember dad and the poachers. Fight! Fight!" he yelled until they twisted her arms and dragged her toward the camp.

The commander called two big boys who carried guns. "Let me hold this!" He took one boy's gun and pointed toward Jason. "Now, Rufu, go on! Eat him!" The boy hesitated. "Yes, eat him! Now! You know, like you did the other Senior-4 boy that went out the back of the bus."

The boy, big and rough looking, with a big head, large teeth, and a weird wobbly look in his eyes, held both hands spread away from his body with fingers grasping air, opening and closing. He came toward Jason with his teeth bared and saliva forming in the corners of his mouth like a mad dog. He grabbed at Jason's arm. Jason snatched it away. But the boy grabbed again and caught it, pulling it, trying to bring it close to his teeth.

Jason twisted and moved to free his arm. He quickly put his body in a whirling football move, slung his weight on the boy. It was a force that twirled Rufu's body so that he almost fell to the ground. He regained balance and came after Jason again, unsteady, staggering, charging. Jason went down low under him as if in a soccer challenge and brought his head up under his chest, giving Rufu a header under the chin. The boy's arms closed on him and his weight brought them both down. They fell to the ground together, and the boy's teeth snapped to and fro trying to bite Jason's hand, but he succeeded in grasping a chunk in Jason's arm. Blood shot out along Jason's wrist. Jason's fingers grabbed the boy's jaw, but Jason's fist and fingers landed inside his mouth. Jason's feet kicked up, like he was playing soccer. He got free of the boy and stood away, whirling his body and bleeding arm.

To the side, Jason saw Katura stamping her feet. When she saw the blood, she yelled, "No, Jason, they are many. Don't fight. Biraro waited and won. Stop, don't fight them now."

Over his anger and desire to show them he was not subdued, the voice of reason from Katura and the memory of Biraro saying "Be patient and wait" cooled him. He stood indecisive, panting, his chest rising and falling spasmodically, blood running from the teeth gash in his arm. He couldn't let that pass. He had to show this boy some things. He stood waiting, then crouched.

The confused commander looked at the passing cars. One taxi slowed down, almost stopping. "Just bring the girl and he will follow. We will take care of him inside."

Jason stood still, panting and yelling encouragement to Katura. "I hear you. You are right, but we will fight them." He followed as they pulled the helpless girl through the banana field into the woods.

A short boy or man met the commander near the edge of the woods, gesticulating with hands and arms. The commander gave him a key to the bus and said to him,

"Yuri, drive some miles away and park the bus in the bush. Take a taxi back here. Don't let people trace you."

Jason watched the short man and noted that he could be the twin of Tempo. The little short man ran to the bus, got in, and the bus moved away while the new unhappy, reluctant recruits were ushered into the bush, guns at their backs. Jason nodded. "Yes. Those two are Pygmies that somehow got recruited to help the commander."

The newly made trail went through a banana field. It ran right up to a stand of mvule trees, close to a young forest of poplar and eucalyptus trees. To the side of the trail, another dented, blue van-type vehicle was parked with hood up and back doors open. A huge, newly built bamboo cage stood near. Made for the transport of wild animals, it was strongly constructed, completely enclosed with a gate of bare flexible branches knotted and knitted together. The door swung open and closed.

The commander motioned with raised beckoning palm to two big boys with guns. Rufu came but the commander waved him away refusing to return his gun.

"Right now, you don't measure up!" he said harshly. "You can't even bite. So how can you shoot? Rejected until you prove yourself."

He selected two other boys, who came running with the guns bobbing up and down, pointing first to one person and then to the sky. He caught one boy by the arm. "You point your gun at his feet." He moved the gun so it pointed to Jason's feet. "Point your gun like this at his head. Like so, and shoot."

The boy started fumbling with the trigger.

"Not now. But if he moves, you bloody well shoot him. If he tries to escape, shoot him. Shoot the gun the way Tempo taught you. You are soldiers now."

The boys stood with the guns trained on Jason, nodding their heads up and down. Katura yelled, "No, you aren't soldiers, either. You're school boys." She looked from one boy to the other and glanced at the commander, who watched her. She frowned a bit, then said, "You both must be about a year older than me, not higher than Senior-1 in school, not soldiers at all. You can't shoot him, no matter what anyone says. Jason, don't you try to run, now. Please listen. Stay there like Biraro. Wait patiently and obey."

Jason realized escape was impossible. Biraro had escaped from the rear door of the bus. He stood and waited, seeking a way out.

When the others were in the cage, the old woman from the bus seemed to fit in with the commander's people. She was one of them for now. She drifted on back with her backpack and packages of meat and teas she had bought at Mbuzi town. She went back by a path where the second van was parked with its doors open, where Jason could see a table and two or more chairs and women moving about near a fire.

The old man was pushed down to sit on the ground beside the commander, who had taken his place on an unfolded chair beside a small table that now held his battered briefcase.

The commander questioned the old man, throwing out phrases in different languages. He greeted the old man in Kiswahili, Bakongo, French, and a few words in Portuguese and Luganda and Bacholi. He listened for the old man's answers. Jason knew that most of the children went to school and understood English. The commander must have been searching for an interpreter who could speak to any adults who wandered into the camp.

This old man was assumed to know all of the different languages of the area. He kept talking to the commander in different languages. So he planned to use the old man as his personal interpreter wherever he went. The old man was clearly frightened, jerking his head, looking over his shoulder constantly.

Three more big boys of about eleven or twelve years were recognized as new recruits with guns. They fingered them with so much amazement at their new power. They ran up and down in the clearing and ventured into the bush beyond, pausing to take cover behind trees and to point at imaginary enemies, shouting and pointing their guns at trees and people. They didn't yet have bullets so they kept sounding off: *"Pow! Pouf, Bang! Biff! Wooom!"* and other explosive sounds. They were acting like this since they stepped off of the bus, even before the commander put guns in their hands. Jason thought they couldn't wait to shoot anything that moved.

The commander, whom everyone now called "Munonga" or "Big" or "Boss," ordered Tempo to show the recruits how to shoot, then stationed the two who had been ordered to guard Jason to stand near the road to warn the commander if anyone approached. "I don't know how long we can stay here before we are discovered," he said to no one in particular. Jason thought the man must be reminding himself. The commander then sat down to question Katura and Jason.

His chair rested near the open hatch of the faded dun-colored wrecked van that was dented and scarred front to back. The hood was up like someone had been working on the motor. Looking inside from the back, Jason saw stacks of rifles and handguns and what must be were boxes of ammunition. One box was hanging open, revealing rows of gleaming shells of different sizes.

When Jason was brought near Munonga, he could see far back behind banana plants and the clearing and the van. There was a cleared area where three women gathered next to a wreck of another van, once blue but now white and gray with a brown tint like camouflage clothing. Someone failed to blend the paint with the terrain. Near a table under a tall tree, a smoldering fire burned where the women were cooking, and the odor of *posha* and scorched millet assailed his nostrils. He saw what looked like a fishpond or a small lake in the background.

A short woman, about the size of Yuri and Tempo, came bobbing out in a sassy dance, flouncing her skirts. She whirled and set a mug of steaming tea on a stool beside Munonga, who playfully caught up her hair. She tapped his face and bowed several times in his direction.

Munonga then busied himself fingering and checking a cell phone that was old and grimy. Jason thought it must have been the same cell phone that he was anxious to have charged in the kiosk in Mbuzi town when they first saw him.

The instrument kept sputtering and moaning static. Now and again Jason understood a word or two, and then Congolese music blared. All the while, Munonga kept mumbling to himself. Jason caught a few words: "Expected to recruit all along here, but you don't answer. Not enough help!" He clicked the cell phone constantly off and on, off and on, trying to shock it into acting, holding it to his ear as if he was expecting a message that had not come. He once got a message with a lot of blaring static: "Bombo and Bukavu," followed by snatches of rhythmic Congolese music again and snatches of a description of some place in the Southern Sudan. Munonga spoke into the dysfunctional cell phone. "If you're still in Congo, know I need relief. Have recruits to unload."

With the music, the little women at the cook fire ran up and began gyrating and whooping and making merry sounds. They came up near the big cage of children where Katura was now held snapping their fingers, their faces animated, their bodies twisting to the music, enticing the girl to join them, to dance. Katura didn't respond but said aloud, "Jason, look—old and small?" Jason knew she still referred to the Pygmies. She had never seen grown women the size of kids.

Jason could not understand clearly. From what he had seen this man was a recruiter who went about the country kidnapping young people for this Lord's Liberation Army. This man did not work alone. He had demonstrated such cruelty that showed that if Jason and Katura were still held when Kony and his full crew came they might never get a chance to escape. He did not know what to do to escape, but he must do it as quickly as possible. Munonga was a part of a far-flung operation dedicated to overthrowing and replacing the present government of Uganda.

Jason wondered about Biraro and the driver. Were they badly injured in their escape? Where were they? Had they notified the army yet? He must figure out how he could escape and report what he knew to the police or army.

Now Munonga's eyes stared unwaveringly into Jason's face. "Let me just say I need smart school boys as recruits. You can get special privileges, and I get points in the army. But I don't have time for indecision. Remember that bus driver's head. I have your name and the place where we found you. Are you joining our Lord's Liberation Army?"

"But sir, we were sent by our grandmother, sir. Our mother is dying and our father is dead."

"I am tired of hearing it. I am sick myself of it. Tired of your delaying. Do you hear?" His voice rose in a menacing yell. "You've seen this stick fall." He hefted the stick that had bloodied the bus driver's head. "I'm warning you. Better decide quickly. I see you are violent and want to fight. I am giving you a chance to fight. Join us or else."

He was seemingly disappointed looking at Jason. He shifted his emphasis. "Your sister is beautiful. We have much work for her. She will help us recruit. Many young boys will join because of her." Jason did not like his suggestion. He glanced at Katura.

"She is very young, sir. Our grandmother is expecting us." Jason felt that the mention of his parents dying threw this man into a quandary; so he kept using it and hoped Katura would say the same things. "Sir, she was sent with me to take care of our dying mother."

"Dying! Dying! Your whole family is dying—of what?"

Katura's mouth was open to speak but, frightened, she said nothing.

"But, sir," said Jason, "our father died of the big A and now mother. My sister forgot to take the medicine Grandma said . . ."

The commander held up his hand. "Quiet!" He kicked the backpacks from under the table toward Jason. "Open it and give me the medicine bottles. I know how to find out what your mother is sick of . . . and your sister, too."

Katura opened her mouth starting to protest, but Jason frowned to silence her. He opened her backpack and handed over the medicine bottle. He saw the label on it, gasped, but quickly recovered.

He didn't know until then that his grandmother had put their malarial tablets into the empty AIDS medicine container that had contained their mother's medicine. The label read: "Take three pills twice a day for immune deficiency syndrome disease (AIDS)."

The commander looked at the medicine bottle and shook his head. "Ah, she has AIDS, and what a waste—she is so pretty."

"Oh, I don't have that," Katura cried.

The commander, holding the medicine bottle, said, "We can't put her with the others—they will become sick, too. Put her in one of the small cages."

Jason knew he must get Katura's malaria medicine to her. He helped get her in the cage, whispering to quiet her down. Then he stood near the commander, waiting for his chance. The commander's eyes were diverted as he took sips from the mug of tea. If only Jason were quick enough. *Now!* As he reached for the bottles, one of them fell over, making the sharpest soft noise Jason had ever heard, but that was enough. That low noise drew Tempo's attention. His eyes were everywhere. He gave the alarm, pointing to Jason.

"*Yeehee.* Boss! Him stealing."

Munonga stared intently at Jason. "I thought you were sensible enough. I was set on making you a captain, but you need more persuasion." He took up the stick and pounded Jason on the hands and head before he was able to move or avoid the blows. "Tie him with the bark fibers you use to make the cages."

Jason knew that anyone tied up with bark fibers suffered as the fibers dried. As they lost moisture and dried, they shrank. It would be painful. They became tighter on the arms and ankles. It was a game he and Biraro and other boys had played. When the sun hit the bark fibers, they dried and tightened until they squeezed round ridges on the flesh.

Tempo was a master at it. He had a roll of the bark strips that he had used to tie the bamboo poles soaking in a wooden bowl near the cage. He took his time, tying Jason's wrists together behind his back and then his ankles.

Munonga watched. "Change your mind. Stop refusing. The Lord's Army needs you. Besides I get points for Senior boys who can be leaders." Jason didn't answer. The man stared sternly. "I'll wait and give you another chance. We will see how you like this." He demonstrated to Tempo how firmly he wanted Jason bound by twisting his own hands and wrists while grimacing. "I think you will change your mind and go with us. In the sun, Tempo." He pointed. "Watch me always. Pay attention. Take those good shoes."

Then he realized that the shoes would fit no one in the camp, so he let them stay on Jason's feet. He was glad because he had hidden the paper money Grandma had given him for their transport in the shoes. He hoped that after tying him up they would put him near Katura, but they held him in back of the big bamboo cage. His sister was in the small cage near the logs where they held meetings.

Katura was crying. "Jason, does our church have an army? Do all churches have armies? Can our church's army fight this one? God won't go against His own army? Ouch! These mosquitoes are eating me terrible." Slap, slap. "What do they mean the Lord's Army of Liberation? I am tied up like a slave."

"Please try to wait," he called gently.

Tempo twisted the fibers tighter and tighter so there was no possibility of loosening them.

"I can't wait. I know I am going to die of malaria. Why can't we just pretend to join the army until we get a chance to escape?"

"Just try to be quiet."

Soon the other short one like Tempo, called Yuri, returned. Yuri was smooth faced and had long hair. The two of them were so much alike in stature and movement that Jason thought they must be twin brothers. Tempo liked his handgun, and Yuri did not have time for guns. He went right to work under the hood of the van, tinkering with wrenches.

"Where did you take the bus?" the commander asked.

Yuri laughed. "Back near Goat Village. I parked it in woods."

"Did anyone see you?"

"Lots of people. Yes, everywhere they worry when the bus no stop for them. I drive on fast and then run from woods. I flag taxi. Nobody see. No one knows."

With that bit of information, Jason lost hope of being rescued. It was up to him. He would have to find some way to get his sister out of here. He had no idea how and when that could happen. Maybe he could free himself and run to the road, hail a taxi, and tell them to get to the army or police. To do that, he would have to leave Katura, and he could never do that.

Jason wondered out loud. "What! What in the world has happened to Biraro? That driver must be in a hospital, the way his head was bleeding. Where are they?" he said while testing the fibers behind his back.

Munonga kept listening to the radio for news and calling on the cell phone. But he could not connect. "Don't know where our relief is," he muttered. "They know where we are. Why don't they answer?"

Jason noticed a trail of ants moving in caravans through the plants on the ground. Some ran up tree leaves and branches and quickly came back down. The whole group seemed to be headed back toward the cooking area, but they were curious about him. Several came and inspected his shoe and his pants leg.

Several ants suddenly left the trail and ran up Jason's shoes and went up his legs and on up his short pants leg. Jason loved his short pants. He loved the rough khaki, white-hunter shorts that came down just below the knees and had so many pockets.

He had heard them called "cargo pants" because they had two big pockets front and back, two lower pockets on the legs, and a smaller pocket near the top of the big pocket on his hip. These pants had belonged to his father. His father as a park ranger carried lots of things in his pockets: keys, cell phones, ammunition, wrenches, pliers, small note pads, chits, numbered metal tags, and stubs of pencils. Jason's pants pocket held only a dried Kiwi fruit that he used for soccer coordination kicking practice. He smiled thinking he should have extra medicine there or a biscuit now that he was hungry. He had no cargo.

His skin itched where the ants crawled over his leg. He waited for an ant bite but they just crawled about making him flinch with expectancy. He watched them one-by-one scout up and down his leg. He moved, thinking so to frighten them. He watched, inspected them, and knew they were harmless. He was glad they were not Sifu. He wondered how long the commander had used this camp on this spot and if they had discarded food, for that would attract the fierce ants.

The sun beamed down hot, drawing sweat from his skin but drying his shackles and tightening them on his arms, causing them to ache. He tried to stay still, thinking what he could do. He leaned against a young tree, a sapling with wide green leaves. Ants in great numbers ran up and down the bark. He noticed them looking from the side while his ankles were tied to each other. It would be easier to lie down but he didn't want any big insects to make a home in his pants leg, so he stood for a long time. He wondered how Katura was faring.

He looked up and saw the two boys with guns who had been relieved as lookouts. One was Rufu with the big teeth that had gashed his arm. They were stopped at the tiny bamboo cage looking in at Katura. Rufu reached in, stroking her hair and pinching her through the spaces in the cage walls. "I am coming in there with you, girl. I want to love you now," he said, glancing around for the commander.

"You better not bother her," the other boy warned.

"I am going in and bang that one good." Rufu laughed, showing his big teeth, and moved toward the cage entrance.

Katura yelled, "Oh, Jason. Listen to that. He's crazy!"

Jason prepared himself to yell and roll downhill to his sister's aid. He measured everything according to the lines on a soccer pitch, estimating he was about forty yards from his sister's cage.

"You can't. You better not," he said.

"Why not? You know that's why she's here," Rufu said, pulling at the crotch of his pants "Girls can't shoot."

Katura yelled louder, "Jason! Please, where are you?"

The other boy warned, "You can't. She's got HIV. I heard the commander say it. That's why she's in that cage."

Rufu withdrew his hand and jumped back from the cage. "Oh, hell, HIV? Are you sure?"

"No! I don't have that."

The boys drifted away from her. They pointed their guns at birds in the nearby trees, aiming at them. Rufu acted glad to have his gun back, even if he had no ammunition.

Jason saw the women farther back in the woods on the trail where the other wrecked van was parked. Yuri was working on it, running the motor while playing Congolese music on the radio. He might leave the keys in the ignition, and Jason could use them to escape during the night. He would rev up the motor and they would crash out of this army camp.

The women ten yards from Katura moved in and out of the van. Smoke came from a fire on the fire pit at the ends of the logs where she was imprisoned and brought the wonderful smell of roasting yams. The women bent down and gave her food.

When they finally gave Jason a roasted yam, he wondered how to reach it. It lay on the banana leaves on the ground. He reached up the length of the sapling and pulled it down behind his back. Then he knelt on his knees, able to move the yam with the branch. It was still warm, dusted with ash from the fire. The sweet sugary juices on the skin glistened. Ants tried to claim it, moving back and forth across it but he brushed them aside, and ate the yam and its wrinkled hot skin.

By this time the sun shone directly on him. He closed his eyes against the glare. He remained in that stance for a long time. Finally he drifted off.

The bark fibers tightening on his skin as the sun dried them woke him up. He turned his body away from the sun, trying to shield his bonds from the fierce heat under nearby branches and leaves. He memorized the camp's layout. He tried to think how it would look in the dark.

Mosquitoes punctured his lower naked legs and upper arms. He moved often to dislodge them. He knew they were also eating Katura. He was glad that she had her hands free to shake them off.

He heard Katura calling. "Jason, did you get some yam? I hope you did." She sounded like his mother, wanting to take care of him. Then, "Jason, I need my medicine. The mosquitoes are mean here."

He believed her and knew they would be worse at night when the sun went down. "I got some food, Katura. I am sorry about the mosquitoes. I will ask Yuri to move you. He seems more human than any of the others. You should ask those women cooks to help you. They can move the cage to the sunlight."

Katura still had a necklace of colored beads around her neck, and her head scarf was still laced over her face. She also had a second scarf in her backpack. He talked to her while the others in the camp settled down to a midday nap. The children in the big cage were moving in and out, down at the blue car, eating. They were carrying ears of corn, and he smelled beans and cassava. The commander was in his van eating and nursing the cell phone.

The women who brought the yams to the children came with bowls of water for them. Jason saw them put the bowls down near the cages. He called several times for Yuri. He thought at first that Yuri did not hear. Suddenly, Yuri materialized near his tree. He stood there, listening. Yuri had his head in the air, his eyes directed toward the van with the commander inside. He did not look toward Jason, but his ear was cocked that way.

Jason said, "My sister will give these women her scarf if she can be moved into the sunlight."

Yuri paused and looked in the direction of the commander and Tempo, who were constantly on the cell phone and the radio. He moved Katura's cage.

Jason could see her now. She was about fifty feet away. He saw her lying there, so forlorn with no one near. It broke his heart to see his sister suffering when he could do nothing. He thought of rolling and twisting closer to her, but he'd better wait as she had cautioned, and not draw attention and make matters worse.

Seeing her slumped in her cage like an animal, Jason could not bear it. He looked away to his arms that had a red weeping gash from Rufu's teeth and a deep circle bored into them where the hot sun was drying his bonds, making them shrink and cut into his arms and ankles. His ankles and wrists throbbed.

Katura said, "This is cruel. Please let us go. The mosquitoes are terrible."

Then the commander got up from his place near the van and came over to Jason. He said. "How do you like this?" He pointed to Jason's aching arms. "You could be holding a gun. Now, we have to move you in case large animals come through here at night."

So they moved Katura's cage into the big cage nearer the van and fastened its door so she could not mix with the others. She was still about fifty feet away. Yuri let her have her blanket from the backpack. She lay down wrapped up, but Jason knew the mosquitoes had already infected her—and maybe him also.

But then two things gave him hope: the commander's cell phone did not work, needing minutes, and the old man, uncooperative, knew the area and convinced Munonga to go to a cell phone-charging booth. Jason knew the one in Mbuzi was closed, so they would have to locate another.

Jason felt if the commander ever made contact with Kony or the main group, he and Katura would be transferred and sent out of the country. They must escape now while Munonga was gone. He could roll down to the cages and get Katura out so she could untie him. His mind raced with plans.

Soon Munonga had changed into torn jeans and an old dirty T-shirt and put on a fez. He and Yuri produced two old beat-up bicycles from the van. With the old man accompanying them as interpreter, the three men headed down the road to get the cell phone charged. Jason was prepared to put his escape plan in action. He was poised to act as soon as they rode off.

But as they were leaving through the clearing, the commander shouted back over his shoulder: "Tempo, Tempo, do your job."

Immediately Tempo stationed boys on the log by Jason and said, "If move, you shoot." There went his chance to escape. Tempo ran around the camp, watching everybody.

Hours passed. Jason waited and watched for an opportunity to move, but Tempo was here and there, giving orders to the women in back and all music ceased. He wrestled one boy to the ground and twisted his arms until he yelled in pain and begged him to stop. Tempo asked one of the big boy guards to hand over his gun for shooting in the woods. The boy, frightening young children with the bloody flapping wings of a dead heron, balked. He would not give up his gun.

"The commander, he give me," the boy said, backing away while pointing the gun at Tempo. Tempo knocked the gun away. Then he pulled his handgun from his waistband and cocked it while pointing it to the boy's head.

"Give or die!"

The boy handed over his gun.

In the late afternoon Munonga, the old man, and Yuri rode back on the rickety bicycles in disappointment. Yuri shouted to Tempo, "Closed down all shops. No minutes on phone." The commander tore off his fez disguise in disgust and soon had a beer in his hand. Ignoring everybody and everything, he set to beating boys with his stick and yelling to Tempo, "You know your job! Watch everything."

Jason lay on the warm ground thinking how to loosen the bark strips on his wrists and ankles. It was too much to think anyone would bring him water, but he shouted for it anyway. He had glimpsed a pond or small lake, but it was too far for him to hop or roll to in the night.

As an old woman staggered near him, Jason whispered, "Latrine. Madame, I need to go for a short call."

She pointed to the weeds behind him. "Just go there."

"My hands and feet are tied. Please, water." The old woman ignored that. She put her mouth to the reed sticking from the gourd of beer, her cheeks sucking in beer. She went slowly away, looking toward the commander. Later she brought water to Katura. Aside from the two boys pointing guns at his feet and head, no one came near Jason.

Then Yuri took the older woman on a bicycle to find a phone-charging kiosk and to buy some kind of supplies. Jason watched amazed at how Yuri's short legs were still long enough to pedal the bicycle.

Jason felt drowsy, defeated. He did not know when he went to sleep. When he awoke later in the night, he heard the small people in back near the second van drumming and singing. They played some music on an African lyre and danced. They took boys from the cage to dance before them and with the women by a bonfire in the back. The women tried to take Katura, but Munonga shook his head and ordered them to leave her alone. He then joined them, carrying his folding chair, lighting a pipe, and urging them on. "Again. Do that one once more."

Jason did not know when the dancing stopped as he lay thinking of how he might free himself. If he were discovered in any attempt at escape, his situation would be worse than now. He watched Katura. Since she never changed her position in her small cage, she must be asleep. For a while the singing began again. There were fewer voices so some had gone to bed.

While he lay on the ground, the plan formed in his mind. He saw little things that at first made no sense. He saw leaves hitting him in the face. He saw water dripping on his head. He saw a wide field stretching for a mile or more. All of it was like a half dream, although he knew he was awake.

But he had to stand. When he stood up, he always saw things more clearly. So he struggled to his feet. Even in the dark, he knew the fifty feet he had estimated as short was a much larger distance. It was much farther than he had at first thought from his position to the cage where Katura was imprisoned. All of that suddenly seemed less important to him. In the darkness, he could master that distance. There was some factor more important than the distance.

From one goal on a soccer field to another goal was a great distance, but somehow they rolled and kicked and controlled the ball until they covered that space.

Then it came to him in a flash. He had three goals: one, to get to the cages; two, to free himself; three—why had he thought so often of water?—water was in front of the cages, bowls full of water. He needed water to free himself.

He might be able to hop to the cages, but there were logs and branches of trees blocking his way. And yet, if he picked his way through he could . . . He tried it and fell over into the low growing shrubbery, into the bushes. Hands and arms were important for balance. His were tied and useless. To move while bound as he was, you had to practice and be prepared to roll and be prepared for twigs and branches striking your face hard, near your eyes. He fell, and they did; they struck his arms and face again. His legs got entangled and brought him down among bushes and loose dirt. He got up and hopped until he came to a clear place, where he rolled over and over . . . toward his goal. In his mind he made it a game. How many rolls to the cage? He counted them. He stopped every now and again to make sure the singing and drumming was still going on. It was quieter, as though only one or two were still awake.

He was near the opening to the cage, crawling and rolling. Now and then he climbed to his knees. There was dirt on his face. He felt it there. His arm got crooked beneath him, caught under a branch, but he turned himself patiently and he was free to roll again.

He felt fresh for the challenge. He had slept and in one sense he was refreshed, so he rolled and hopped.

Once the music stopped, the commander would return and discover Jason gone. Nobody came. He heard female laughter and shouting: "Play that again," and soon the drums and singing began again. Softer now, they were tiring.

Jason hopped and rolled until he reached the bowls of water outside the big cage. Now with his hands tightly held behind him, how to do this? He did not know. He had not thought past the point of getting to water with his arms behind him, but now he was here, he turned his back to the bowls and tried to grasp one with his fingers. Sitting back he felt the cool water on his buttocks, realizing he needed it on his wrists.

He grasped the bowl again and held it for a moment, pouring water on his wrists and hands. He raised his legs so the straps of bark touched the water in a second bowl near his feet. A section of the bonds were wetted but the knots were on the other side, still dry.

Desperate, he held a bowl and tried to lean on the bamboo spokes of the cage to scramble and muscle himself erect. He expected some of the children inside to awaken, but he only heard their soft snoring. He did this with the bowl still held behind him. He put his fingers in the bowl and splashed upward, wetting his hands and rubbing his bonds a little at a time until the bonds seemed slippery in places, looser. More water. He worked for some time bringing more and more water to his wrists.

He had been thinking about the knots—to untie the knots—when he should have been thinking of the bonds. Now he felt the ones on the legs loosen from the water, and then they were slicker, so he kept it up, going from bowl to bowl splashing the water. He felt them loosen and soon he could move his legs—those were loose. His wrists slid by each other—he got another bowl and splashed the water again and again, and he could feel his wrists sliding over the slick fiber of the bark where he had restored its slickness, and now his hands were moving and then he felt one wrist start to slip free.

He stopped breathing . . . to listen. There had been some sound . . . near . . . his heart pounded. His chest hurt with the effort. At this moment, Katura called his name louder and louder and would not stop. She kept calling, in her sleep, "Jason, Jason, I am so cold." She was nearby and surely would awaken the other children in the cage.

"Shush. Wrap the blanket around you and try to sleep."

But she repeated loudly, "But I'm cold . . . so cold, Jason. Cold all over!"

He hurried now, hoping no one was awakened by her yells. He was splashing and rubbing his bonds. "Ouch!" He touched the painful wound from Rufu's bite.

SEVEN

JASON WORKED URGENTLY, THEN MOVED to another bowl and frantically splashed water over the bonds that held his hands. His wrists slipped and slid against each other, then slowly freed. He brought both arms around and rubbed them up and down on each other, trying to remove the crevice of flesh that had formed a knot around each wrist. Sometimes he touched the painful swollen gash that oozed pus from Rufu's teeth bites. Jason worried about that. He had heard that people could get a disease—tetanus or lockjaw—from teeth bites.

He was working to free his hands when he moved, rolling his arms, and found his feet moved up and down against the slack, slippery tethers. At last, he could move his feet. Quickly untying his legs, he stumbled to Katura. Putting his mouth close to her ear to whisper, he drew back, shocked. She had complained of being cold, but now, after what seemed to him only a few minutes later, she was hot. Very hot!

He spoke to her quietly, gently shushing her, and slowly drawing her out of the cage. He turned, looking all around them. Here and there, his eyes took in the whole camp: the cages, the path out to the road where two boy guards waited with guns.

He quickly glanced at the van and the guns inside. He found their backpacks and rumbled through them, searching for the medicine bottles. Not there. Probably in that beat-up briefcase with Munonga. He saw guns and ammunition. Guns. He was tempted to take one, but that would make him a soldier. He fled from them.

He guided her, stumbling, almost falling with each step toward the road. He went quietly, whispering to her, propping her up, and propelling her alongside him. His arms felt free and he was ready to run now. He braced for a challenge hiding among the banana trees. He crept up to where the boy guards lay. He rushed to them wielding his stick, ready to challenge them, to jump on them. But the two boy soldiers who had been left to guard the bush entrance lay asleep, with their guns lying at their sides.

Jason stopped, again tempted to take a gun, but it would just delay their escape. He had no idea how to shoot a weapon. He caught up the backpacks, dragging Katura along with him. They hurried through the banana field, the branches of bushes slapping them on their legs, arms, and faces. Katura mumbled incoherently.

They must follow the road, hiding until late in the morning. They ran, panting and stopping every few minutes to allow Katura to catch her breath. Stopping again to listen, he heard his heart beating at his temples like a hammer. He found it difficult to move faster, weighed down by the backpacks and blanket while supporting, almost lifting and carrying, his sister. She was very heavy.

He was so afraid that she would die right there in their escape attempt. Sometimes she was hot to the touch, and at other times, she was cold. This abrupt shift from hot to cold and back again frightened him. What if she died and left him alone? What would he do? He thought of his mother and Grandma then. He heard the echo of Munonga's voice: "*Dying, dying, I am sick of it. Your whole family is dying.*"

He rebelled. My family is not dying. "No we're not." He had been too occupied during the night to think of them, but Katura's illness brought all of it back.

They stumbled out on the road. There were few cars. They ducked back in the bush when from a distance the bright lights of oncoming cars lit up the road. Once a vehicle like Munonga's van slowed down. They hid for a long time. But that car went on, and the road was again in total darkness. They ducked down in roadside bushes, only their eyes showing. Were the commander and his Pygmies out searching for them?

He was thankful for the cars, because they would frighten away any animal predators.

We are running away from people but we are afraid of animals. Back home they had a fence to keep animals away, but it was the poachers who broke down the fences to do harm to the animals. It is always that way—people do more harm to animals than animals ever do to people. The human poachers stole their lamp. Human animals harm and hunt each other and make little children into killers in the name of a church and say it's God's will.

He shook himself, starting to move again. *Now I must focus on our escape. How long until daylight?* The sky was black except for dim stars. He must not stop. Katura stumbled and fell, but he couldn't let her rest. He pulled her up, coaxed her on and on until the moon rose. Its light found them far enough up the road that they could sit down in the tall grass to rest beside it for a minute.

Cars passed, but he was afraid as long as it was dark. If he tried to flag down a taxi, he might signal Munonga and Tempo searching for them. He got Katura on her weary feet again, and they took to the woods along the road until they came to a bog, making it impossible to travel anywhere but on the road. They kept running, falling, getting up, and going on, anywhere away from that Lord's Army. Running and falling and getting up and running until they fell on the ground, exhausted. He would rest for a few minutes. Dozing, he heard Katura softly snoring and calling, "Time for dinner." In his sleep he smiled and raised a hand to wave her away.

In the morning light the song of the yellow and brown warblers awakened Jason. He watched their colorful bodies as they constructed amazing inverted nests. He hoped he was miles from their captors in this peaceful grove. No houses, no Liberation Army. No sounds of cars, although they were still near the main road, the one which led to Grandpa's.

He could hardly move although there were no bonds on his arms or legs. He stretched his limbs. Then he took off his shoe and pulled money from his socks for the taxi fare to Grandpa's. Katura lay beside him, wrapped in a blanket, shivering sometimes and then suddenly freezing. His face creased with worry. But they were free. He had to think carefully of what to do next.

EIGHT

Jason was determined to ride in a taxi instead of a bus, for he feared the Liberation Army would take over any bus he rode. He hid Katura in the weeds by the roadside and stood waving for taxis to stop. Several drivers stopped, then went ahead quickly when Jason stepped behind a bush to bring out Katura. Jason knew from their quick acceleration they were frightened. They didn't want to take into their taxi a sick person or anyone that might present a problem or die in their car. They had probably had the experience of people dying in their car.

Then Jason pleaded with Katura to act more lively. "I know you are sick, but try not to show it until we have the ride."

"I was hot just now, but oh . . . so cold now."

"Don't worry. We'll get to Grandpa's soon."

Finally, they were given a ride in a taxi van. Jason was lucky, sitting in a rear seat where no one had to pass in and out by them. They could ride this taxi all the way to Grandpa's little farm on a side road about three miles from the nearest town.

"We'll soon be there. Grandpa will know what to do to help you. He will have some quinine or some malaria medicine from the Shelsia Clinic in town." He rubbed her head. "I know you will soon feel better, Katura." However, he was worried that his sister might not recover. He had heard stories about people losing consciousness, going into a coma, and never waking up.

Their driver distracted Jason, waving to other drivers going in the opposite direction and trading for some green corn or tomatoes or roasted meat.

Once, some boys came to the car window selling roasted corn. Jason bought a cone of roasted nuts, still hot, and waved them under Katura's nose, attempting to wake her and have her eat them, but her eyes were closed. She shivered beneath the blanket as he held her. He studied her, especially the splotches and welts of mosquito bites, swollen and grayish on her face and neck. He was afraid for her. He had never witnessed sickness like this in a young person. Katura's illness almost matched that of his father and mother. It was bad. He'd bet it was the worst kind of malaria. What if it was mixed with something worse?

For the fifth time he searched through their backpacks for the medicine, but that army commander had taken it. Anxiety rose up in him when he thought of the taxi drivers who had refused to take them as passengers. Did they see something that told them Katura was near death? He looked closely at her face again. Did she look like Daddy? No, Daddy was sick with a different disease for a long time before he wasted away. He didn't look like anybody—he had just vacated his body before he left them. Katura was still here fighting it. He hoped medicine, food, and rest would save her.

The drivers who had refused them a ride were afraid Katura would die in their car. What if Katura died in this taxi . . . in his arms? What would he do? He hated Munonga, Tempo, and Yuri, and their cruelty to lock her in a cage. Where were Biraro and the bus driver now? Why didn't they come back to help?

He glanced out of the window at the trees and banana and pineapple fields along the road and prayed that Katura wouldn't die. He promised God he would be more kind to her, more protective, and not say hurtful things. Jason's mind went to work on what little science he knew. Mosquitoes were vectors. They carried little animals in the glands in their mouths and when they bit you, they spat the poison out into your blood. *Oomph!* That was disgusting! How did God make such creatures as mosquitoes and that Liberation Army crew?

His mind returned to his studies and the plans for the future that he and Biraro shared. Next year in school he would have a chance to expand his knowledge. He should have paid more attention when the science and history masters talked about disease vectors. He was thinking of experimenting on animals with herbs and medicine right here in Uganda. He thought of his Grandpa's friend, Mr. Kasamba, the village medicine man. He never knew exactly how much of his herbs and roots to give but Jason wanted to make his medicine exact. He and Biraro might study abroad but they would not remain in America or England or India. If they went, they would study and come back, and do medical research right here at home.

Most students went outside of the country. When they gained an education, they stayed out and had luxurious lives, and their children grew up in England, France, or the United States. That hadn't helped his country. But they could have the same type of life here in Uganda.

Bouncing up and down in the taxi, he remembered talking this over with his grandmother.

"I'm not sure you can do research here. I prefer that you become a medical doctor."

"Why not? I read about Pasteur and Madame Curie. They did all kinds of research, and Pasteur did it on animals."

"Tradition—I think is the European word. And another word is superstition. I see the puzzled expression on your face, baby, but the Europeans had it, too. It's taken them a long time to get it under control."

"How does that keep us from doing research here?"

"The traditions of clans and their totems will make it difficult for you. Special animals and plants have been important in some clan histories, and they will be angry if you experiment with them. More importantly, these people will not use medicine made from their totems' hooves, fur, hair—or from special plants. These offended people won't use herbs that might save their lives if the medicine comes from a family totem like mushrooms."

The trip took most of the day. The road passed through a forest where trucks were loaded with eucalyptus logs for a mill, then through hills and hills of banana plants. Toward evening, as the sun made its way through the tall trees on the left side of the taxi, they came to flat land. Through the dusty window he saw the banana trees giving way to coffee and pineapple fields. There was the sign for Nanansi, the town near Grandpa's farm, near enough to reach before nightfall.

When the taxi came to the town, he looked out the window and hardly recognized the place, it was so changed. In the dark, it seemed the trees and houses were closer to the road. He hesitated to tell the driver where they should get off. The driver stopped near two different side roads before they found the right one with the grove of trees Grandpa had planted when Jason was born.

People still moved up and down the road on bicycles and motor scooters, carrying bags and baskets of goods. Some carried firewood and water pots on their heads. Jason saw those entering houses alongside the roadway where smoke rose from the kitchens.

NINE

JASON DID NOT RECOGNIZE THE place at first, because it seemed so much closer to the roadway than he remembered it and because there was a jeep and a big troop transport truck parked in the yard and the nearby field. These blocked him from seeing landmarks that he ordinarily would have remembered. There were two tall soldiers standing outside holding guns at the ready, and Jason saw several other soldiers getting up from the back floor of the big brown military transport truck. No one occupied the jeep. Grandpa emerged among the soldiers squinting at Jason and Katura.

"Heh, heh? It's you, Jason! And you have brought little Katura with you!" His voice was soft as he wrapped his big arms around them.

The Uganda government soldiers, holding guns and other weapons at the ready, snapped at attention and retreated two steps back. Relief and joy flooded over Jason, as if a giant boulder barring his way had been shoved aside. All at once he felt lighter.

"Come on, boy, bring the child.

Grandpa picked up Katura in his arms. Inside Jason saw soldiers sleeping on Grandpa's living room floor. There was Biraro, fast asleep.

His grandfather gently laid Katura on his bed. He was busy feeling her temple and rushing in and out to the kitchen, bringing water and shaking medicine bottles, holding them up to the light.

Then Grandpa rushed to the kitchen to make sure water was boiling, and he brought other medicine bottles from another room. He was holding up Katura and patting her face and gently crooning to her like Grandma did to their mother back home. He was slowly waking Katura.

She blinked, looked up at him momentarily, and closed her eyes again. He kept calling her and telling Jason to hold the water while he used a teaspoon to grind up a pill into powder. He poured water on it and then took up Katura's head again and talked to her gently, forcing her mouth open with the full medicine spoon. Some medicine ran from the spoon over lips and on her blouse while he cajoled her to cooperate.

"You sick baby, let Grandpa help you. Just open your mouth a bit . . . No, no, don't bite the spoon . . . or turn away . . . Now . . . you have to take this . . . you are very sick!"

He pushed the spoon into her mouth. She looked at his kind, friendly face, opened her mouth to breathe and to greet him. Then he emptied the medicine in her mouth. More medicine and water ran onto the sheets. After Katura slumped over asleep again, Grandpa covered her.

"Poor baby, I wish your grandmother were here, but she can't be everywhere at once."

Jason could not contain his concern. "Will she get better?" He needed his grandfather to say something positive.

"The medicine will have to do its job." He studied Jason, smiling. "When you arrived, I thought you were your daddy. You have grown so like him. I have been hearing it all from your friend Biraro there." He nodded toward the sleeping friend. "He's completely tuckered out. His lieutenant says he hasn't slept in two days while they searched for you and Katura. He has so much news for you. I'm glad you came before he has to leave. We heard about your trouble from him. He has been sick and recovering from falling on the asphalt out of the back of that bus. These are terrible times, but we got our own army right here now. So we don't have to worry."

But Jason did have to worry. What did he mean about Biraro leaving? They would plan for the next school year and travel home together. It was safe now. "Have you heard from Grandma? I want to know if that girl went to help her. Our cell phone never worked, and we have not been in contact with her."

"Several times, worried sick. She blames herself for sending you and Katura out alone. After your friend Biraro called his sister who was helping her and reported your kidnapping by the Lord's Liberation Army, she was more upset. I'll call her in the morning to tell her you and Katura are here with me." He hugged Jason. "You are tired and should sleep now. Katura will be better soon."

Grandpa looked at her, worried. "We need to take her to Grandma's clinic." She had been involved with the women of Nanansi in setting it up, but it was the Women's Community Clinic—that was the real name—but everyone knew it as the Shelsia Clinic. Jason was sitting in the big chair in the living room watching his friend sleep, and he drifted off to sleep while listening to Grandpa. He wanted to question Biraro. What did Grandpa mean, he was leaving?

TEN

WHEN JASON WOKE THE NEXT morning, someone was poking him with a military baton, repeating a familiar question. "Do you want to be in this army? Say yes and I'll make you in charge of all the breakfast millet." A smiling Biraro jumped on top of his friend yelling, "Now, watch me, Tempo." He was laughing so hard he slid to the floor.

Most of the soldiers, except for two soldier guards left outside, were eating their breakfast in the bed of the truck, their rifles near them. The rest were scattered all over the house. Grandpa was helping to serve them food from his kitchen mixed with their own army rations and mangoes, pineapples, and melons.

"Wait! Wait!" Jason yelled, raising his hands to pause the celebration. Then he ran into Grandpa's room; he had to see Katura first. She was awake, being tended by Grandpa's neighbors: Old Mr. Kasamba, the medicine man, and his wife. Katura was being spoon-fed from a bowl of steaming millet. They were gently forcing on her slices of baked cassava and yams. He touched her warm cheek.

"We're here, and you're a bit better."

He smiled at her. She pointed weakly to mosquito bites on her arms, fell back against the sheets, and closed her eyes. Mrs. Kasamba would not let her sleep; she urged her to take more food. He looked at her for a moment, comforted that she had improved overnight. Jason went out to join the others at breakfast.

Biraro grinned. "Jason man, you made it. I knew that Munonga couldn't keep you. All you had to do was be patient and wait your chance. You gave me that signal to go out the back just like we did in the soccer games. Remember that! No one could block you. That commander is an animal. He had kids biting and eating each other alive. Look at my ear!" He turned his head to one side, cupping the damaged healing ear in his hand." The top edge was missing, covered by a brown scab. "That boy with the slobbering mouth is sick. He almost bit my ear off."

Jason showed his wounded arm. Biraro compared it to his almost-healed ear. Then he said, "We have been everywhere up and down this road. We followed you through every *shamba* and banana field after someone reported the bus parked near Mbuzi town."

Biraro led Jason over to the man dressed in a smart green uniform. This officer had just returned in another jeep from a neighboring town. "You must report everything to Lieutenant Ndugwa. He needs to debrief you."

Jason wondered why Biraro was talking government language. "*'Debrief?*'" What was that about? Why did he want Jason to talk to an officer when Biraro had already told him everything? Jason wanted to talk about school and their chance to talk to Mr. Kasamba about herbal medicine. He wanted to just forget that Lord's Liberation Army and Munonga.

Biraro said, "We need to know what happened to you in that camp. How many people were there? Did they communicate with anyone? We need a description of everyone, their vehicles, and anything about the commander's boss, that Kony. The entire army and neighboring countries are searching for him all over the continent. It will help us to find his gang."

Jason was surprised by Biraro's bossy attitude. He didn't understand how he had suddenly become a stranger. He acted like an investigator, talking like he was in the army.

Biraro led him up to Lieutenant Ndugwa, who had a mouthful of flat, yellow cassava cake. He chewed with his mouth to the side and said to Jason between bites, "Aha! You're the one who refused to join the Lord's Liberation Army on that bus. Biraro told us about you and your sister." He looked closely at Jason, inspecting his arms and face. "Except for that one healing bite, your arms are clear. How did you escape the eating? They tell me they have biting matches, and the one who does not say yes to them is eaten. Look at Biraro's ear. Is that how you got that scar on your arm?"

"Well, the man in charge had his hands full with us." Jason half laughed. "He was frantically trying to get in touch with his leader, a man named Kony. But his phone wouldn't work. We didn't make things easy for them."

"Oh, yes, Kony is the one we're after. He's a bad case." He looked around. "Did you happen to get his cell phone number?"

Jason shook his head.

Lieutenant stood up and shouted, "Hey, everyone, the latest from our outpost: the Liberation Army is getting money for food, supplies, and guns from the poachers. The money is coming from abroad, and so are the guns. We don't know what country, where they sell the poached animal parts. You know rhino horns, elephant tusks—ivory is at a premium now—but the guns come in through the Congo. We must treat both gangs as one threat."

He turned to Jason and said more quietly, "We found guns and ammunition in that blue battered van where you and your sister were held in the woods with the others."

Jason was amazed to learn that Liberation Army was connected with the poachers who had robbed his family home and stole his mother's lamp. He shook his head in wonder. Biraro paced and talked rapidly, opening and clenching his fist like Jason used to see him do in a tough soccer match when they were losing.

"That driver that fell out of the back door of the bus with me broke his arm. We had a hard time getting a taxi back to Mbuzi, and then calling for the army and taking him to the hospital. Lieutenant Ndugwa came with his squad. We searched all along the road all night. Early the next morning we spotted two kids along the road with guns. When we burst in there, the commander and most of the others escaped down a back path.

Biraro shook his head to remove the fear. "That Tempo nearly killed me. When they first came to our house, I knew right away they were that scary army. Tempo makes you think he is one of the boy recruits, but he is a well-developed man who can wrestle like fire. When I said I wouldn't join them, he put me in a headlock and nearly broke my neck. Then they threatened my family. He said he would use my sister to recruit men and boys. He threatened to take us all if I did not join him. So I told Mbabazi not to worry and I quickly joined them." Biraro rubbed his neck as if he could still feel Tempo's arms. "He nearly killed me with that hammerlock."

They went on talking about the rescue, and how Jason had escaped from his bark cuffs.

Grandpa came out from Katura's room. His face was lined with worry. He spoke to the lieutenant. "There's a clinic in town where my wife used to work. We should take the child there. I would feel better if the nurses looked at her. Mr. Kasamba says we should not try his quinine medicine at this stage. The girl is still critical."

The lieutenant had just returned from town and planned to order his men to break camp after breakfast. "Of course, my driver will take us. In my absence the men can pack their gear for our departure. We must be in Masaka by nightfall."

They all packed into the jeep. Grandpa gave directions to the main road and into town. They parked outside a low, squat building of cement blocks. There were several houses, a car garage, a blacksmith, and the herbal medicine shop with a glass window displaying skins and medicines.

Two young women in blue uniforms and starched white caps met them at the door. They were escorting patients out, a couple with two small children and bags of medicine. The tall nurse, whose serious manner reminded Jason of his grandmother, excused herself and accompanied the people outside. The other one greeted Grandpa and immediately began chatting with Katura, holding her hand, feeling her temple, and looking closely at her eyes.

"Your grandmother has been calling for us to get ready for you. Please sit here." She put a thermometer in her mouth and read her temperature. The other nurse came in and talked excitedly to Grandpa, who introduced the lieutenant.

Above the examination chair Jason saw a photo of Mrs. Hillary Clinton posing with her daughter Chelsea and the community women's group. Mrs. Clinton had spoken to the women's group and had so impressed them that they raised the money to fund the clinic by selling goats and other produce. They named it after Chelsea Clinton, but now it was called the Shelsia Clinic. According to the BBC news, Chelsea in America was married now, expecting her first child. In the photo Mrs. Clinton held her book, *It Takes a Village*. The village women built this clinic.

While they were looking around the clinic, Grandma called and wanted to talk, first to Grandpa and after that to Katura. Jason heard her warm voice on the speakerphone and rushed into the room. He listened with his ear close to the phone, saying yes they were fine and at Grandpa's, and yes they were together. And then Grandma was all advice.

"Katura, you better listen to me. Cooperate with Grandpa and Jason and take your medicine. You must stay there until you are well and strong. At least three days there, do you hear?"

And then she talked to Grandpa again and made him promise to keep them until Katura was completely well. Jason was concerned because Grandma had not said anything about Mama and the baby. But they had hung up.

Jason was eager to talk to Biraro alone. Here they were at the clinic near Mr. Kasamba's shop. They had made their pact at Grandpa's during the holidays when they were in Senior-1. Now they were in Senior-4 waiting for O-level exam results. They had to be sure about their future plans.

Jason saw warnings on the white walls in English, in the vernacular Runyankore or Kiswahili:

CAUTION–YOU AND AIDS
MOSQUITOS KILL

MALARIA AND STAGNANT WATER
WASH HANDS

The short nurse showed them the small room with cabinets of stacked clean towels, sheets, and gowns. Cases with stacked gowns and pillowcases lined the hall. They passed an examining room and two rooms, empty except for a chair and a bed draped with mosquito netting, ready for an emergency patient.

In the hallway they saw the small, locked, glass medicine cases with bottles and pill boxes. Then the tall nurse called for help, and together they carefully took Katura into the shower. The nurses soaped and scrubbed her, cleaned her, and gave her a change of clothing from the clinic. Katura looked weak. But Jason was happy she was so much improved. Once or twice she even smiled.

The two friends walked out into the hall. Jason nodded his head in the direction of the herbal shop across the road. "We were going to experiment and standardize the herbal African medicines that Mr. Kasamba showed us. We can go and talk more with him."

Biraro looked away, uncomfortable. He wore a khaki cap like those worn by soldiers. He removed it and wrapped it around his hand. "We don't have time, the unit is moving as soon as we get back. I must go with them." He nodded his head back in the direction of Lieutenant Ndugwa. "He should take you also. You have valuable information for the country."

"But that's why we have an army to find people like that."

"But eyewitnesses are always important."

"Why can't they take the bus driver?"

"They will, but he was sick when they started out. Now that the army is ready to give chase, they need my eyes."

"But why? You don't have to go. You can stay here with us and travel back with Katura and me."

Biraro looked away. "Jason, didn't you hear what the lieutenant said? I have to go with them. I am the only one beside you who can identify those army people. They are running about the country, trying to regroup, darting into the Congo, or crossing into the South Sudan. This unit is chasing them as they move from country to country. I heard a lot when I was taken by them. I have to help."

"Biraro, we're not soldiers. You are just a schoolboy. You can choose what you want to be."

"Not anymore I can't. This thing has taught me that sometimes life chooses for you. I have already joined the Uganda Army." He shrugged. "I have to go for training. After those beasts came and threatened my entire family—they took me and beat up an ordinary bus driver—I have to make a stand."

"You joined the Rifles?" Jason shook his head in disbelief. "What about medicine?"

"Now my path is different."

Jason stood there frowning, with his head hung low over his chest. He shook his head from side to side. "I heard the lieutenant. I thought he was saying you had to leave with them. I hoped it wasn't true."

"Someone has got to stop this Kony. Right now you and I are the ones who can identify the commander. The soldiers need our eyes, and it's going to be a long fight. I have got to help." He wrung the military cap.

"Others can carry guns."

"We are needed at this moment. We picked medicine, but the protection of our families is more important. Children forced to be soldiers, I can't live with that. I know you will see it. This Lords Liberation Army is a sham, a con as dangerous as any disease spreading through the country like TB, Ebola, AIDS, and malaria. It is destroying the peace of our country. People are kidnapped from their homes, and children are given guns and taught how to kill each other. It is another disease that attacks all of us. This vermin steals the life of young children. I saw kids who were taught to attack and kill each other. We saw them made to bite each other to death. You saw him beat a public servant, a bus driver who was doing his duty taking people to a real church on Sunday morning. This thing is evil."

"In study hall we talked of the future. We made a choice. Don't you remember our field trips to the Virus Research Center at Entebbe?"

Biraro nodded but did not say anything.

"Don't you remember what the institute director said to us before we left? He said he'd noticed how attentive we had been all during our visit, and that someday students like you and me would take his place. Remember that?" He looked at his friend with this blazing memory in his eyes.

Biraro reached out his hand holding the army cap to touch his friend's arm, the way they used to do during a soccer match. Jason jerked his body away, tears flowing. He wiped his eyes with the back of his right hand and saw at the same time the gash ripped in his arm by Rufu's teeth. He turned away in anguish and frustration.

"Oh, Biraro. We could have . . ."

Jason stood by the door and looked out across the street. He glanced back angrily at Biraro once or twice. Suddenly, he opened the door and ran blindly outside. He didn't know where he was going. After crossing the street, he stared into the window of Mr. Kasamba's shop.

There were the dried herbs that he planned to study in his future lab. He would discover the chemical compound and then the dosage in the mushrooms that cured diseases. He would study the quinine from the cinchona bark to treat the malaria patients. Scientists like Madame Curie and Pasteur had worked hard and followed their dreams even when no one believed what they were doing was important. He wondered about the compounds in the cured brown leaves or the balls from the gum tree that young children were given to chew when teething. He was curious about everything. There was so much unknown that he needed to know.

Then he ran along to the jeep and sat in back, with the silent driver at the wheel waiting for the others. He wept bitterly into the sleeve of his shirt.

ELEVEN

Jᴀꜱᴏɴ ᴡᴀꜱ ꜱɪʟᴇɴᴛ ᴀꜱ ᴛʜᴇʏ drove back to Grandpa's. He was glad that Katura was the center of attention. He pretended to doze off in his corner. The lieutenant had received new orders, extending their leave to the next day. Jason waited, hoping for Biraro to come and talk with him, but neither boy sought out the other.

They discussed the visit to the Shelsia Clinic. The lieutenant told Grandpa he was impressed with the nurses, the care, and the building. As the army units moved throughout the country, it was comforting that such a medical facility existed here. Jason didn't take part in these discussions. He looked out the window, seeing nothing, hearing nothing, lost and forlorn.

The nurses came early the next morning to look in on Katura and, of course, to see all of the young men and to wish them well.

They examined Katura, took her temperature, and said she was on the road to recovery from her battle with malaria. They visited with Grandpa, talked briefly with Grandma on the cell phone. Then parting with smiles and jests with the young soldiers, the young nurses reluctantly rode away from Grandpa's house on a motor scooter. They had other calls to make, taking medicine to families in the neighborhood.

After their talk at the clinic, Jason and Biraro avoided each other. Jason was surprised at the attention Biraro was paying to Katura. He sat in a chair near her bed talking to her. Jason noticed the two of them fell silent whenever he came by the door. He had never thought of Biraro as having a particular fondness for his young sister.

Jason still thought of her as his baby sister, although he had to face that she was growing up right before his eyes. He had been disturbed by two boys making lewd remarks in front of the cage where she had been held. Munonga had planned to use her to recruit soldiers.

Now he'd seen his sister and Biraro in Grandpa's room, heads close together in a secret moment. They moved apart and started talking about Munonga questioning her on the bus. Her answers, even in such a threatening time, made Biraro laugh.

"I'm sorry to hear you will be joining the army right after you get your O-level results."

"I am already in the army. Soon I report for duty. I will hunt down the people who harmed you."

Jason was listening. Biraro was trying to raise himself in his sister's eyes as some kind of hero. At that moment Jason did not regard him as a hero. He saw him as someone who could not keep a promise.

He fled from them. He spent the rest of his time talking to the young soldiers, who asked him questions about how he got out of the ties of bark fibers in the Lord's Army camp. He had played with these soldiers as kids. He answered their questions while avoiding Biraro.

After the soldiers left, Jason walked about with Grandpa in the fields looking at the ripening pineapple plants and plums. Mr. Kasamba joined them.

"Jason, I expected you and Biraro to come and talk to me about your studies and your plans after the O-level exam results."

Jason did not know how to talk about his breach with Biraro. "He had to go with the Rifles, but I still want to talk to you about medicine."

"So this is a good time to come with me for another look at the cinchona tree, if you're still interested in studying herbal medicine."

"Sir, I am very much interested and excited. I want to see the trees and watch you make medicine. But I am sure you have heard that Biraro has joined the army."

"Maybe in the future he'll return. Have you heard about the discovery of an oil field near the lakes? Now there will be more scholarships, more chances to study outside of Uganda. Some members of parliament are petitioning the president not to sign any deals with the foreign oil companies until they agree to put a refinery here. If that happens, they will have to build an oil research laboratory as well. Many medicines are made from oil. Come along, I am going to cut some cinchona bark. Do you want to help?"

Jason knew about Mr. Kasamba's woods but he'd never visited. Medicine men usually had their children or somebody important in the village to mentor. Mr. Kasamba's family had been decimated while he was outside the country studying. He had no children or close relatives except his wife, who had studied in England with him.

Jason followed Mr. Kasamba to the end of the pineapple fields and into the woods until they came to a dry hilly area where in a small glade of trees a spring bubbled and threw clear water upward in a weak spray. The spray fell noisily over some shiny rocks. His eyes followed the hills upward and in the distance was the clear face of a rocky mountain. It seemed close, though its distant peaks were glazed with snow.

"Sir, what's that mountain called? I didn't know from my geography lessons that we had any mountains this close."

"It's the Ruwenzori, the 'mountains of the moon,' and it does seem close, but it is far away."

He pointed to the spring. "This water comes from the mountain's snow. Feel how cold it is. The melt runoff from the mountain's snow comes to us in an underground stream. Most of the water for the village and the town comes from that mountain."

Jason looked to the left of the spring and saw Mr. Kasamba's lab consisting of tree stumps and logs arranged as tables with buckets and jars set on them, covered with burlap sacking. There were his tools, a saw, hammer, axe, chisel, and a hand drill with a grinder attached to one end. The herbalist showed Jason how he ground medicine, heated, and then distilled it.

He was amazed that Mr. Kasamba could produce useful medicine with such crude equipment. Many people suffering from malaria or diarrhea had been cured by his preparations.

Mr. Kasamba took an axe, made two small cuts to loosen the gray-green bark, and removed it. Jason took over the work. When the bark almost filled a five-gallon oil drum, they covered it with spring water.

"Jason, the water is clear now. We will see if there is any change tomorrow."

Mr. Kasamba opened a box of the dried medicine sealed in bottles or wrapped in bark or banana fibers. Jason listened, thinking about the laboratory at school with its shiny tables, faucets, and glass beakers and flasks. In his mind, he transformed Mr. Kasamba's workplace in the woods into a modern lab with Bunsen burners and test tubes. He and Biraro would measure and purify medicine and make pills with accurate milligram dosages.

He turned to Mr. Kasamba. "You said the members of parliament want to make the oil companies build a refinery. Would they build a lab like the ones at school or at the Viral Institute in Entebbe? Would it only make products from oil like gasoline and kerosene?"

"Yes, of course, that would be the aim of the oil companies to make a quick profit. But many medicines come from oil. The process releases substances from the plants and animals that created the oil. These byproducts could be analyzed, isolated, and identified as medicines. That's the kind of thing that you and Biraro were planning. You need to know that everything in science is connected to everything else."

"Sir, how are you able to do it? Isn't the cinchona somebody's clan tree, a totem?"

"*Eyieee*, Jason! Where did you hear that? You have been listening to old people. Yes, many animals and plants are sacred to special clans and tribes. First, let me tell you that the cinchona tree is not native to Africa. So it is not a clan totem. It was brought here and cultivated just as some food plants were introduced here by people who migrated here in recent times. The cinchona was brought for medicine from South America."

"My grandmother says that it will be difficult to research medicine here using animals and plants, because families have mushrooms, grasses, lions, and muskrats as totems that they are sworn to protect and never harm."

"That's true, Jason. Your grandmother is right. But most modern people don't even know their totems or the histories of their family origins."

"Grandmother promised to tell me about the story of the mushroom clan."

"I will tell you. It is the totem of the ancient king Kintu's family. Each clan has two totems, a major one and a minor one. On the morning after the burial of an ancestor, they found his grave covered with mushrooms. Since that time it has been their honored totem. People are allowed to eat mushrooms, but I don't know how they would react to your experimenting with them. Most people are loyal to their traditional king. It would be very dangerous to offend a clan."

Jason said, "But that idea is primitive and stands in the way of progress. Everything we use comes from someplace else: the Boda Boda from Dubai, solar panels for cell phone towers from China, shoes from England."

"Your grandmother's solar lamp was made by a young African in Kenya. The country and the world are changing. We've come a long way from listening to your transistor radio while you took care of goats."

Now Jason was more determined to pursue his idea of learning how to discover and refine and do research in medicine right here in Uganda. He followed Mr. Kasamba to his lab in the woods for three days, and at the end of that time he knew how to make quinine and had a sealed bottle in his pocket. He noticed Katura was getting better every day.

One day he passed near his grandfather's plum orchard where the fruit was ripe. He was excited because Katura loved plums. He pulled a handful to share with her. He wanted to speak with her and get ready to return to Grandma. He had to know that Katura was back to good health and ready to travel. For the last few days she had been quiet, and they had not talked the way they used to. She seemed more reserved. He wondered about what had passed between her and Biraro.

◆

Twelve

Katura loaded the cloth bag Grandpa gave her with plums from the trees planted the year Jason had been born. Whenever they came during plum-ripening season, they ate many. They always took a bagful home.

In a shed beside the orchard, Grandpa showed Jason two bicycles. One was fairly new and lightweight. It was the one Grandma used to ride to work at the Shelsia Clinic. Now that she wasn't home, Grandpa rode it to the store. The heavy bluish-gray one leaning in a corner was for a long time Grandpa's main source of transportation. He carried bunches of bananas, sacks of beans, or coffee to the market. He no longer did that but instead hired a truck. Cobwebs waved from its heavy frame. This machine was sturdy like the ones used by workers on the road for transporting tools to work along small paths where wide roads had not been built.

Jason grasped the handlebars and pulled it out. He had seen men carrying beds, doors, and windows strapped on it. At other times he witnessed the transport of several sacks of beans stacked atop each other on the carriage seat along with several bunches of bananas slashed to the sides. He remembered seeing an entire family, a man with two children and a mother, perched on the carriage seat, on each other, and on the handlebars.

It was a bicycle that could enable a family to live in the bush where there were only paths big enough for people to pass in single file. Jason sat on it, balanced, and rode on it a short distance, wondering if he could pedal this bicycle most of the distance home. It could get them home faster if he could balance Katura and their backpacks. In his mind he could see them rolling up and down hills.

"I see you're looking at the master cycle," said Grandpa. "Well, it takes a strong man to pedal it uphill, but yes, it could carry you and Katura home. You are filled out and muscular like your daddy. If you two stayed another week, the pineapples would be ripe enough to sell, but since we're unable to reach Grandma on her cell phone, you should be getting back. Or I could load the bicycle with bananas. You could sell them and ride the bus when you get tired. I promise you will get tired."

Jason took the bicycle outside, wiping away cobwebs. He tested the brakes. Satisfied they were fine, he ran his hands along the wheels' spokes, checking the firmness. His fingernails made soft music against the metal spokes as they zoomed by his hand. He smiled and turned the bike upside down, seat on the ground. Next he turned the sprocket, sending the wheels whizzing around. He felt the tires: they were fully inflated.

Grandpa knelt beside him, showed him the tire pump attached to the frame. "You can always put air in a tire. You can roll up to any village shop and get a tire patched or repaired in a short time."

Jason flipped the cycle upright. He felt its weight, which would help going downhill. He nodded, thinking of balance. He sometimes rode his dad's bike that was of the same type. He touched the light on the side; he pushed the little switch. The light did not come on. It had no batteries now. Grandpa didn't see the need of a light since he never traveled by bicycle at night.

They decided he could do it. Together, they oiled it, wiped the dust off of it, and got it ready for them to leave.

Grandpa loaded the carriage seat with three bunches of bananas and tested it by sitting and balancing them. He watched Jason ride up and down, fast and slow, to see if he could balance the load.

"Just sell them at the first town you come to. The sixty shillings will come in handy. Then you'll have only the weight of you and Katura."

Katura had the plums and the box with Grandma's lamp, wrapped in the sleeping blankets that Grandpa gave them to replace the ones they had lost.

Now Jason could see that old Grandpa was sad to see them leave. He followed them from the house to the pasture among the goats to the graveled road that led to the big road where they would start for home. Together they lashed Katura's bundle on top of the bananas on the carriage seat.

Grandpa looked intently at both of them and patted Jason on the shoulder. "You're the image of your father." He hugged Katura close. "Now that you are healthy and fully recovered, take the lamp to Grandma."

Jason started out slow, feeling the weight of the loaded bicycle wobbling beneath him if he favored either side. While his feet pushed on the pedals he was balanced and the bicycle did not require much guidance. Katura sat far back on the seat leaving room for him to rest his back. He spun out on the road.

There was hardly any traffic this time of the morning, a few taxis and pedestrians headed for market to sell pineapples, peas, or corn. Women with flaring skirts carried huge baskets on their heads, and men with the circles of grass balancing long entire bunches of bananas trod along the side of the road. The spokes in the tires of the bicycle sang and hummed along the road as they picked up speed. Jason had learned to go as fast as he could downhill and then use the momentum to carry up onto the next hill. A few times he had to swerve to avoid a pedestrian who appeared suddenly from a settlement or a car that took up most of the road while taking on passengers.

The sun threw its rays through the mimosa and eucalyptus trees. The spokes of the bicycle hummed musically under them.

"Don't forget the minutes," said Katura, reminding him about the cell phone.

"Yes, I know. When we sell the bananas we will buy them."

When the smooth tarmac road flattened out, more people thronged the road. A town must be near. There were fields of millet and pineapple and beans. They passed a school, a hospital, and a bank. Jason pulled his bicycle up where many peddlers waited with carrots, tomatoes in bunches still on the vine, papaya, and chickens and goats, all for sale.

They watched the passing people. They had stopped in the front of the city market, but they had no time to go in.

When Katura reached into her hair, Jason teased, "Yes, that's right, you can bring out some money from your private bank. Take this cell phone to that booth over there and put some minutes on it."

"How many minutes?" Katura asked.

"Twenty shillings' worth. How much money do you have?"

"I don't want to tumble all of my hair and look a crazy girl. I have only this five-shilling piece."

"Well, I have some money Grandpa gave me. Here are fifteen shillings."

Katura started away toward the booth.

"I'll be right here waiting for you," he called after her. He watched her until she was talking to a man at the cell phone booth who took the phone, opened it, wrote something on paper, and held out his hand for money.

"How much each?" said a man in long pants and a *kitenge* shirt, looking at Jason's bananas.

"Thirty-five shillings each," he said, remembering what his father had said about bargaining in the marketplace. "*Never at first tell your exact price, say a little higher. Then you can wait and reduce it to the price you really want.*"

"Surely not! How can you ask that much?"

Another man in shorts and pushing along a bicycle said, "How much is the boy asking?"

"It's disgraceful. He is asking thirty-five shillings each."

The second man slapped himself on his leg, "Impossible! He will take them home again. Nobody will pay that!"

Jason thought the two were friends but trying to play a joke on him. He had seen this happen with his grandfather. He said very quietly as though his confidence was shaken, "Then how much do you older men think I should be asking?"

They glanced at each other quickly, walking around looking at his bunches of bananas. "You might be able to get fifteen shillings each for them."

Jason shook his head. "My grandpa said thirty-five."

The man looked around. "Is he here?" He glared at Jason, "I said, is he here?"

"Who?"

"Your grandpa isn't here. Nobody here will give you thirty-five shillings each."

"Well . . ."

"Come on," said the man. "I haven't got all day. Reduce your price."

"Thirty shillings, then."

A crowd had gathered. Jason saw how the man impatiently moved his feet from side to side. He really wanted the bananas. "I'll pay twenty shillings each or you can keep them."

Jason looked over his shoulder through the crowd of shoppers and peddlers for Katura. She should be back by now.

The man stood in front of Jason so he couldn't move. "All right, twenty-five shillings each." He counted the bills into Jason's hands and untied the bunches of bananas from the bicycle.

Jason was worried. His sister had not returned. She wasn't in the line at the cell phone charging booths. His eyes searched through the crowds. No Katura.

A boy approached, sliding watches up and down his arm flashing silver and gold in the sun. "Just twenty, see how they shine. You always know the time. No longer look at the sun, instead look at your arm. School or shop no matter. It doesn't scold when you ask. Silent, you read the time. Buy yours. It will fit your arm. All right, how about fifteen? I know you have it, you made big sale." He held it up in front of Jason.

Jason liked the look of it; he would love to hold his arm up at school and flash his watch in the faces of the surprised boys or girls there. He clenched his teeth, shook his head. He didn't need a watch. He needed his sister so they could continue the journey back to Grandma. It was a long way and now it was nearly noon. He pushed his bicycle up, lighter without the bananas and waited in line near the cell-phone recharging booth.

Someone said the Chinese solar panels were restored, so the prices were higher. It was a trick to get people to need their phones very badly. He listened to the complaints and waited. He had to wait until three customers were served.

"My sister bought minutes. Have you seen her?"

"I don't know your sister."

"She had a ranger cell phone, a government type "

He nodded, "Yes, I saw her. Someone was selling—" Then the man abruptly turned to serve a customer who was complaining and in a hurry. He turned back to Jason. "—bracelets and scarves, colorful, shiny things. I didn't get a chance to charge her phone. She went there." He pointed with his nose away toward the shops.

Jason pushed his bicycle toward the shops. Among the crowd of shopping, moving people he knew no one—women with babies on their backs, men with satchels, peddlers with baskets of food on their heads. Many people who walked by held live white-and-brown chickens. Goats bleated in the backs of trucks. Motorbikes passed with women passengers dressed in short or long skirts, sitting sideways on carriage seat as the drivers maneuvered their way through the crowds on the street or sidewalks.

Jason recognized no one. He thought of calling out to her, but what was the use? It would only serve to broadcast that some vulnerable person was missing. He stood in front of the shop for a long time. He must wait near the place where Katura had left him or they would never find each other again. And he couldn't go into the shops looking for her and leave the bicycle.

Then he saw a young woman with a lot of scarves flung across one arm and a line of bracelets on the other. He saw something that frightened him. She carried a cloth bag stained with plum juice, Katura's bag of plums. He pushed the bicycle in front to block the girl's path. He grasped the bag. "If you don't answer me, I am going to call for help. Where is my little sister?"

"I don't know you. I never saw your sister."

He caught the girl's eye and held it. "Do you know what this crowd of people will do when a thief is caught? They don't ask questions. They throw stones until you're dead. I am going to report you as a thief. This is my sister's bag you are carrying. Where is she?"

She still hesitated.

He put a hand toward his mouth. "I will give the *ndulu*, the alarm for thieves." He waited. Her eyes told him she understood: if he made that sound everyone in the market would come to stone a thief. Fear rose in her eyes.

The girl tried to free herself and throw the bag down. "Please sir, I was helping your sister. Don't report me."

"Where is my sister?"

Desperate with fear, she tried to break away, but Jason held on to her. "I helped her to find a latrine. She's there. She's coming." The girl pointed toward the back of the shops.

"You took her money for your bracelets and scarves, then stole her plums and ran away. We will wait here for her."

"I am not a thief. Please, sir, I just couldn't wait for her near that latrine."

Several minutes later, Katura came out through the crowd. She was worried, searching among the crowd of shoppers and peddlers, but her face brightened when she saw her brother. "I had to go to the latrine after that long ride. This girl helped me. Then she disappeared."

"Where are the bracelets and scarves you bought? And why is your hair all undone?"

"Jason, I am sorry." She looked at the scarves on the girl's arm and took several. "Where are my bracelets? Did you steal the bag of plums from Grandpa?"

"I was keeping them for you, and I found your brother."

"You didn't find me," said Jason. "I found you escaping after stealing my sister's money. Now, Katura, take what is yours and let this thief go so we can get home."

Jason bought them a Fanta soft drink and sat on the bicycle in the shade of a mvule tree until Katura had plaited her hair and tied her head in a scarf. Jason wanted to criticize her for using money to buy scarves and bracelets when they needed the money for transportation. But he had been tempted by the watches and had nearly been persuaded to buy one. He had resisted, proud of his self-control, mature enough to follow his grandmother's advice to think before actions, to see more clearly the consequences.

THIRTEEN

THE BICYCLE HUMMED UP AND down hills, around curves; the black tarmac seemed endless. They passed a small settlement of houses near a river famous for big perches. Here most people caught and sold fish, either from the lake or from ponds where they farmed them. All around, the land was green and the forest grew thick and tall. People lined the roadway into town, and there was a big school. Jason had planned to spend the night here. They had passed here with their father on the way to visit their grandparents. It was not safe to travel further in the dark.

He was still angry with Katura and he did not talk to her. So with no one to share his doubts, he pressed on past the town where he would have ordinarily spent the night in safety. When he looked again, the sun was almost setting. On each side and all around them were sand and palm trees. In the distance he saw here and there a stand of baobab trees.

Suddenly, a herd of zebra sprang across the road, their hooves kicking up whiffs of sand. Farther along, several gazelle bounded across in front of them.

When the family had traveled here when his father had been a game ranger, he remembered his father saying this area was a migratory path that animals took yearly, going from forest to plains. The area was not safe for pedestrians.

Katura's hands shook as she held onto her brother's waist. He ferociously pedaled the bicycle on and on.

"Jason!" she screamed. "Is it safe to travel at night here? Do you remember what father said about this place?"

She had been ten years old and still remembered their father's words. She must be wondering if leopards and lions were hungry, humans could also become their prey, their food.

He kept on pedaling.

"We'll stop at the next town," he said. But where was the next town? As they went ahead, the sun dropped farther down behind the trees. Few cars passed. Packed taxis sped away from the desert.

Katura was shaking. "I am afraid. Let's flag one of these taxis. They can put the bicycle on top, and we can ride. You have money to pay."

"I'll do that." he said, pedaling as the sun hid itself in the palm trees. No taxi passed.

"What are we going to do?"

"Just be quiet. It is really your fault that we are out here at night. You delayed us when we were getting the cell phone minutes and selling the bananas."

She didn't say anything, but he saw she was so frightened that she was shivering.

Jason kept pedaling, expecting a settlement of houses, any dwelling, to pop up along the road. But it was desert and all they heard were crickets, the drone of other insects of the African night, animal noises like hyenas, and a few wild desert birds flying by them on the way to roost.

Then suddenly ahead in the dusky evening, some figures loomed. Jason saw a parked Land Rover as the bicycle rounded a curve. He was going too fast to make an instant decision. He started to slow down, wondering what to do. His first impulse was to turn the bicycle around as fast as he could and go back the way they had come. But then he saw people in the road blocking his way. They looked friendly, signaling him to stop.

He stopped in the middle of the road. There were three men: one in the middle of the road with short khaki pants, a wide brimmed hat, and a bandolier with bullets or cartridges across his shoulder; and two others near the parked Land Rover with the hood up.

He had made a mistake stopping here and started to pedal again. The man grabbed the handle bars.

"Friend, I say, chap, do take it slow. We are in a bit of a stew and need your help."

Jason remembered the slang from British hunters who sometimes visited his father's ranger station.

"Friend, friend," echoed the others, moving toward the bicycle. The first man wore a baseball cap turned backwards, a *Been There, Done That* T-shirt, and green khaki shorts with *Down* printed on one leg and *Under* on the other. "Just wait. Now, be a good bloke. We are in trouble here and need your help. We'll pay."

"I have no 'elp. We must get on 'ome. Our parents are waiting for us in Rendutu," said Jason, speaking like an Australian.

"Ah, but Rendutu is far. You won't make it until daybreak. Might as well stay and help. Two punctured tires, and we need to go to our home—some miles."

The other man was a light-skinned African. *Not from around here*, Jason thought.

"How could I help?" Jason asked. He was nervous.

"Bombo, you tell him we are friends." They would think he would trust Bombo because he had darker skin, more familiar.

Bombo said, with gestures of familiarity, "If you let us use your bicycle, I will go there to the village a few miles away and bring a fundi to fix our tires. We pay you. You spend night safe."

"But we are already late."

"Listen! I tell you—very dangerous. Rendutu, too far."

Jason looked at the three men. All were tall and strong. Probably they could run faster than he could. Katura was clutching his sides and shaking. He was one against them.

The Land Rover was brown with black lettering like zebra stripes: *Been There! Done That!*

"Let me and my sister talk alone," he said, his voice shaky. They held the bicycle, and Jason pulled Katura aside. He could see she was relieved since they had found other people instead of animals, but he was not convinced of their safety.

He held her arm tightly. "We have no choice but to let them use the bicycle, but we must stay together no matter what and be ready to escape if we get the chance. Don't talk to them. Just keep quiet no matter what is said."

Bombo was already mounted on the bicycle. The Australian whispered to him, "Matey, bring the big Land Rover."

Then Jason said, "We need our sleeping bags and goods." They gave him their things from the carriage seat of the bicycle.

Bombo pedaled away at a fast speed, going on a side road no wider than a footpath. Jason looked in that direction as he drew his sister near to him. But he saw no living creature. The landscape was dark with no light anywhere.

No cars passed along the road. "It is as though we left the main highway some place back there, but I think this place is so desolate that no cars venture out here at night. They all stop for the night in some village instead of crossing here." He talked on trying to make his sister comfortable.

"What was that one whispering to that Bombo about?" Katura asked.

"Something about a big Land Rover."

The Englishman tinkered with the car radio, the Australian collected grasses and used a machete to cut limbs off a fallen tree. With branches and brown dried leaves, he started a fire alongside the road. "That will discourage the wild animals, mate." He nodded to Jason before using a cigarette lighter to light the fire.

The two men lighted a cigarette, puffed, and passed it between them, talking and laughing.

Katura moved near the fire and covered herself with a blanket. The men kept tinkering with the motor of their vehicle. One of them announced the headlights were out. "There must be a short from when we hit a rut."

Jason moved near to Katura and whispered, "Do you see those pieces of burning fire wood? We must plan to defend ourselves. If they become violent, we will use the firewood and hit them or burn their car."

"But if we do anything, they may hurt us."

"They may try to hurt us anyway. We can't make it easy for them. Understand? You must fight."

"All right."

Above the night noises, they heard the Australian and Englishman talking quietly.

"That's why we must get the tusks to Rendutu no later than tomorrow."

The other said, "Capital! Yeah, that's tops for meeting Bombo and the tanker driver Abdul later tonight."

"Sure they don't meet anyone with the load for Bukavu."

Katura's eyes were open. She wasn't sleeping, too afraid. He brought her close to him for protection. He had trouble staying awake. Pedaling all day up and down the hills with no food had exhausted him. He dozed off. She woke him once, poking with a finger in his chest to give him a plum, which he nibbled. Before he could finish it, he was asleep again. She shook him. "You can't sleep. You don't know what will happen."

Later, Bomb's return in a larger Land Rover roused him. Four men were loading something that looked like small tree trunks, hurrying in the lights of the vehicle. They had brought tires for the lame vehicle, but Jason did not see his bicycle anywhere. The new bearded man was quickly changing the tires. Jason started complaining loudly.

"Where is the bike? I want our bicycle."

"Your bike is at our camp where you must sleep tonight. Don't worry, chap. Everything is capital as I told you. We can't let you go now. It's too dangerous," said the British man.

"You can't hold us here. You said if we helped, you'd let us go."

"Your bicycle is safe. Come and eat a meal with us. You must stay here with us until daybreak."

Bombo and the other bearded one called Abdul left in the loaded vehicle. Then the Australian and Englishman ushered Jason and Katura into the back of the smaller vehicle and drove back onto the side road through high grasses and bush for several miles.

Fourteen

Jason and Katura bounced up and down in back of the Land Rover, surrounded by sealed wooden boxes, guns stacked in one corner, machetes clanging underfoot, and a sewing machine case. The vehicle bumped over ruts until they came to an odd line of eucalyptus trees out in a palm grove.

The headlights revealed three brown tents strung together along a sandy flat area. As soon as they parked near a transport truck, three women came out of the second tent. Dressed in local clothing from different parts of Africa, they greeted the men, held their hands, and embraced.

The Englishman said, "We've guests for the night, and you girls be hospitable to them."

"Are they men or women or both?" the one named Sonia Kabala asked. She wore a colorful cloth draped attractively around her shapely body and a turban wrapped Egyptian style around her head.

"No, they are two children. Teenaged boy and a girl. Bombo should have told you when he came for the tires."

"Well, Bombo was only in and out. I guess he's rushing to meet his sweetie in Rendutu. Never even stopped to eat the deer meat we'd baked in that gas oven."

"Venison, my dear, not deer meat. That makes it sounds crude, unappetizing. Say venison, that's what you'll hear in London or Sydney. 'Venison is roasted, dear.' Not 'Deer is roasted, honey.' Although you might hear that in the States."

"You girls never were outside Nairobi. You should come to a sheep station in the Big Country."

One spoke proudly in Kiswahili. "Me? Dar es Salaam and Nairobi. Nobody is ever going to see Markia in Down Under as you call it. Dar es Salaam is my home, and I am sorry the day I left Dar. I must tell you I am not suited to the bush. If you leave me here again like this, I won't be here on your return."

"Where will you go, Markia? What transport will you use?" said the snickering Australian.

"We were prisoners when you were gone."

He kissed her. "Yes, you're my prisoner. Don't you like it?"

She answered him with more kisses.

One man brought out a knife to open a can of beans to go along with the brown, glazed venison and from some hidden source produced sliced pineapple, a round melon, boiled corn, and a canister of salt.

Jason and Katura sat at a small table near the door so they could see their bicycle. The men had no further use for it. The Moslem man, Abdul, was busy tinkering with the lights of the Land Rover and checking the tires.

Jason wandered outside away from the tents. He wanted to know everything about any place he stopped, especially where he was captive. He was satisfied this area was high and dry, and there were no mosquitoes. But he knew now that this was a poachers' camp, and he needed to find out more about them while making sure that the poachers didn't figure out that he suspected them.

Abdul rubbed the outside of the motor with a rag moist with gasoline. He threw the rag on a pile of paper and rags. He held a limp cigarette between his lips, struck a match, and lighted it, tossing the match down near the pile of rags.

Whoooom!

Suddenly, there was a flash, a sharp smell of burnt gas. The match lit a spot on the ground and flashed to the rags. A blaze flared up, the rags burning. Abdul looked all around, startled. He stamped the fire out and beat it with a bush. Worried, he moved his gas can a safe distance away from the still smoldering rags. He dropped the cigarette in the sand and stamped on it several times.

Yasmin had her dark hair in a beautiful scarf and wore a sari. She did not speak much, greeting Abdul with a bow, her hands in front of her chest, her eyes smiling.

They showed Jason and Katura to the center dining tent. Katura and Jason ate at the small side table while the men were served by the women at the big table covered by an elegant tablecloth and napkins. The women served beer and whiskey to the men and sat with them, kissing and laughing.

The Australian came over to Jason. "We said we'd pay you if you helped." He handed him twenty-five shillings. "Is that fair, mate?"

"Yes, but can we go, now?"

"No, you must stay until it is light in the morning. We'll take you back to the highway." He patted Jason on the shoulder. "The lass looks pert."

Katura said, "Better eat a lot, Jason. You are already slimming. You slept like you were dying. I need you to eat more. You don't know when we will get food again."

She was hiding a piece of pineapple and meat in her blanket. She reached for another ear of corn, but a hand closed on it before she could claim it. She made a face when Abdul, who sported a dirty black beard, put his greasy stained nails and hand into the food trays on their table. He wiped his sweaty face with his hand. No one challenged him. Katura push her food away in disgust.

When the candles had burned down, they unrolled the blankets. Jason saw a machete rolled into the blanket. "What's this? How did this get there?"

"You said we might have to fight them."

"When did you get it?"

"You were asleep by the fire and so were the other two. One of us had to stay awake in case of trouble. When that man cut trees to make the fire, he left one lying on the ground and I took it. You told me we had to fight, and I was getting ready."

"Wow, Katura. That was a great thing you did."

"I was scared. What now? We have to sleep."

"They are just poachers. We can leave here as soon as it is light."

"Poachers?"

"Yes, that's why they have a camp here where the animals cross. They kill them and make trinkets from the animals' parts for the tourists or send them back to England, Australia, and the States. All they need is a hunting license as long as they stay away from restricted areas, such as the game parks. They can catch any animal they want."

"Jason, how do you know that?"

"Father used to talk to Grandpa about it. I heard them when we passed here once. While we rode in back, I opened a box full of ashtrays, belt buckles, and slippers made of elephant feet, leopard skin, and other animal parts. That's what this camp is about."

From their assigned sleeping space in a small alcove, they could see the interior of the dining tent and the women's work area beyond. It was empty now. The men had hoisted the giggling women in their arms and carried them off. Now Jason heard the clink of bottles and glasses from the far tent.

He studied the guns in the corner similar to the ones used by Munonga. Alarmed, he realized that the poachers supplied them to the Liberation Army. Another disturbing thing: the tablecloth with the hibiscus flower design and tear on the edge was identical to the one his mother used to have.

Then Katura pointed. "That looks just like the lamp the poachers stole from our house."

"Sleep now. I'm waking you at the first light."

He must call Grandma as soon as possible to notify the army. If he hadn't been so angry at Biraro, he would have the phone number.

At dawn, Jason woke Katura, who demanded they take the lamp. He reluctantly agreed. They crept outside and rolled the bike away from the camp. Often they looked back over their shoulder to see if they were followed, but Jason reasoned the liquor and the female companionship had tired the poachers.

Finally they reached the main road, and Jason began to pedal with energy. Soon they were being passed by trucks and cycles, and pedestrians appeared. The sun beamed down—they were free again with the morning air striking their faces.

FIFTEEN

THE TWO TEENAGERS EMBRACED THEIR freedom with joy and sped along the tarmac ribbon. Katura repeated how happy Grandma would be with two lamps instead of one. She pinched Jason's side and yelled, "Grandma can choose by which lamp to read old dull medicine bottles. Now I need food. Jason, don't you get tired and hungry smelling it all along the way? But we are eating little snippets of leftover pineapple. I was going to take some venison last night until that Abdul with his sweaty beard hanging all over it and his old nasty hands came in just when I was about to wrap it up. He was gross, admit it. Say it out loud! And stop grunting. Talk or something! Stop and let's eat, then we can talk, and you can do your practice. I'll give you a plum, or you can buy a kiwi to use as a practice ball."

Katura went on talking, and Jason went on pedaling and not stopping. He knew she talked to pass the time. Her voice was rhythm to keep going up and down hills.

He listened, pedaled, and paused in long coasting rolls downhill, feeling the wind over his head and the soft ripple of the tires moving over the uneven roadway. He stopped only once in the shade of a matuba tree shading the roadway, pausing on a slope so he would not have trouble starting again. He stretched his legs and walked a few paces up and down, breathing in and out as they did in physical exercises at school. His sister stretched and shook her legs, searching for a food peddler.

Then Jason was calling her, anxious to get started. "We must be sure to not repeat what happened last night. Let's go." They coasted down the long hill, and Jason began pedaling again, flashing past people, plantations, markets, and gas stations. The sun swept across the sky while the sweating boy pumped down the road and the girl talked.

Toward evening, the road under the bicycle tires rushed alongside banana plantations where sturdy brown houses stood in the green landscape, their corrugated tin roofs gleaming in the afternoon sun.

They had long since eaten the chunk of pineapple that Katura had wrapped in their blanket. They had stopped for a drink of water at one village where young girls carried pots on their heads from a nearby borehole. While young children sang, danced, and wove circlets of grass to steady the round-bottomed gourds on their heads, Jason and his sister pumped water for them. He invited them to splash pots of water on his sweating body until it shone and glistened in the sun. His clothes were wet but he felt relief. He repaid them by swinging on the borehole handle until their calabashes gurgled full, splashing over.

Katura danced or helped the young girls with their weaving and decorated their lithe bodies with vines and flowers. They showed her dances from their villages until Jason yelled impatiently for her to jump on the bicycle again.

Now they were on the move again, and Jason was very hungry. They flagged down a bus and put the bicycle on the rack. Katura's words of the night before came back to torment him.

"*Eat a lot. You have to work hard pedaling the bicycle.*" He wished he had eaten more.

From the shops alongside the highway Jason smelled roasting meat and baking corn. Katura, sitting in a seat on the bus just in front of him, smacked her lips. "Do you smell the food?"

"Every time the bus stops to take on passengers, a crowd of peddlers come to shove the meat and roasted corn in my face. I can hardly stand it."

"Well, let's buy something, I'm starved."

"I'm not going to make the mistake we made with those poachers. It is getting toward late evening. We should stop for the night at the turnoff for Mbuzi and the ferry. Then we must get off this bus. It's as far as we have paid to come."

"Can we get food now?"

"We can find a place to sleep and start fresh tomorrow morning. We will be home the day after tomorrow evening."

"I hope we can sleep. I have slept very little. That woman put her noisy baby in my lap and told me to hold him. He squirmed all the way and peed on me. My dress is still wet and it stinks." She flipped the hem up and down in an attempt to dry off.

The bus was stopped to take on bananas, the driver bargaining and having big bunches stored on top of the bus. He laughed, showing his stained teeth, turning his head to avoid the thin spiral of smoke from the stub of a cigarette lit between his teeth. He seemed glad Jason was taking down his bicycle. It gave him more space to put up baskets of corn, rows of pineapples, and sacks of green cabbages to be sold in the next town.

Traffic was heavy, trucks and taxis going the other way or parked for the night.

This town was set at a junction where several roads joined from the mountain. Jason thought one came from the lakes where Mr. Kasamba said oil had been discovered. A few places had signs up advertising rooms. They had to find a very cheap and safe place to pass the night. He pushed the bicycle off to the side of the road, out of the way of cars and pedestrians near the shops. They paused and watched the owner ladle white sugar into brown paper bags on a scale, put down tea, a bag of corn meal, and several cassava roots while his nimble fingers moved over a cash machine totaling up the cost.

Dusk was settling in the valley while sunshine still lit brown big-horned cows grazing on hillsides. Spicy aromas filled the air. A young woman with a red-and-blue bandanna wrapped around her shoulders turned samosas, a mixture of spicy ground meat and chopped vegetables covered with batter. Dark brown corn sizzled on a brazier. Jason bought two ears of corn, three samosas, and a bottle of Fanta Orange to share.

"Jason, let's ask if there is a safe, cheap place where we can sleep."

"Who can we ask?" he said, looking around cautiously. "We should not let strangers know we're traveling alone."

"We shouldn't have to be afraid here, since we are near to home. Any minute we may see someone who knows us."

"Well, we're not that close. Let's be careful. You never know what may happen. You go and ask that woman who just sold us the food where we may sleep tonight. Better hurry. She's wrapping up her things, getting ready to go."

Katura laughed. "She's no woman. She's not much older than me. It's getting dark. I hope we can sleep early and long." She handed her bag to Jason.

She went back to the girl, who stopped her hurried effort to close her business. The girl talked to Katura, pointing down the road where he saw the highway sloping downhill with fields of bananas, millet, and cassava on each side, a few trees, and many fast moving cars on the road.

Soon Katura hurried back, excited and smiling. "I was right. She is a girl in Senior-4 just like you, taking O-levels next year."

Jason was amazed that so much information could pass among women and girls in such a short time. Boys would take days to exchange that much personal stuff.

"She said her mother will gladly let us stay. It will be not more than three shillings."

"Where is it?"

"Along this road just a little way."

"That's good to get away from this busy marketplace where cars may be stopping all night."

Cars, trucks, bicycles, and Boda Boda scooters loaded with people waving and gesturing were passing them. Horns blew, brakes squeaked, and loud drivers ordered people to stop or go. Several heated arguments flared, protesting delays.

Jason placed the girl's bundle on the bike. He pushed the loaded bike while the two girls followed, chatting and giving directions. Both girls wore short dresses and low-heeled shoes. He wished he could study the girl more closely.

Smoke issued from chimneys, and now and then the sound of drums or flute notes rose through the banana fields. Boys drove a herd of goats along the side of the road, swatting their legs with tree branches to keep them away from fast honking cars and shouting people.

White clouds raced across the green hills, as a big yellow moon, almost full, rose. Houses pushed away from the road back into banana farms, among papaya trees, holding close to fields of cassava plants.

The girl turned in toward a house where smoke rose from a chimney at the side of the house.

"There's mother now."

A woman moved among pots and pans on a table made of bamboo strips. *Again, food,* Jason thought. Hunger rose in him with the scent of cooking plantains simmering in smoldering banana leaves and peanut soup.

Under the darkening sky a continuous line of trucks, taxis, cars, Boda Bodas, and bicycles rushed toward them. These vehicles chased each other down the hill at terrific speeds.

"Yo!" Jason said to the girl. "This is a dangerous place! These lorries and cars could leave the road and end in one of the houses along here."

"Ah, *bom, bay!* That very thing has happened. Two months ago, a truck ran off the road among Mr. Kamoga's goats in the pens behind his house." She pointed to a house next to the one they were about to enter. "It was late at night. That truck barely missed our house. It killed three goats. That is why a wide trench is dug along the highway there. Mr. Kamoga, a government official, insisted that the PWD protect his house and property. Everyone along here is grateful to my father."

Jason remembered he had not reported to the government that group of poachers because his phone was not charged. Now he said to Katura over his shoulder, "Perhaps we should tell this Mr. Kamoga about that group of poachers that held us all night. Until now we have had no chance to report them." Actually, because of his quarrel with Biraro, he had pushed away its importance.

Katura nodded and began telling her new friend about how they were captured first by the Lord's Liberation Army including grown men only as tall as young boys. "You could see they were older and cruel. A large boy bit Jason, like a mad dog."

The girl approached him and patted his arm while she studied his face.

Katura continued, telling about the mosquitoes, and she admitted how she had refused to take her medicine and how she eventually suffered because of her stubbornness. The girl's eyes were soft with sympathy.

Jason told a short version of how they had been confronted by mixed people on the road, and then escaped. "I say mixed because they came from different parts of the world, Australia, England, Africa, Dar es Salaam. Oh, and some part of the Arab world. Anyway, they turned out to be the very poachers who robbed our house in the canyon near the game park and stole our mother's lamp. They're now friends and allies of the Lord's Liberation Army, probably supplying them with guns. I know it sounds weird. Now we have the lamp they stole from our house. It was in their camp on the table where their girlfriends served us food—where Abdul's greasy, dirty hands and scraggly beard made my sister too sick to finish eating."

The girl was so amazed at the story that she stood still along the busy roadside, frightened, a hand over her mouth. "You must tell Father at once, so he can get that information to our official army."

"That's what I plan to do," Jason agreed.

As they talked, more cars swerved near them. Katura screamed when one truck braked sharply and almost turned completely around, nearly blocking the roadway. Cars squeezed

by each other, barely escaping a catastrophe, slowing briefly but
never stopping.

"Don't be frightened. They can't cross that ditch, but they
do crash on the other side at night. Father says the road curve
is too sharp for their downhill speed."

The mother met them at the door. "Selina, did you bring
the chili peppers?"

The girl handed over a small brown bag of spices. "Yes, and
also black peppers."

The mother poked her nose in the bag and smiled and
pulled her nose out sneezing and dabbing at her eyes with the
corner of her apron. "Yes, and it's hot. I like that, good for the
vegetables." She looked at Jason and Katura. "Who are your
new friends?"

"No, Mom, they are customers, school kids like me. Just
traveling about, on their way home. But they need a place to
sleep tonight. Can they sleep in my room? They will pay three
shillings."

The mother looked Jason and Katura up and down. "Two
shillings each for the night. You are just in time to join our
evening meal." She looked at Katura's hair. "What's happened?
Is that how you started out from home?"

"No, then it was in basket weave."

"Well, what happened? This girl is too old to go about
looking like she has no mother."

Katura turned away embarrassed, fussing with her hair.

"Never mind, after supper I'll do yours like mine," Selina
said, turning and patting her nice, high basket weave. Katura
smiled in admiration. Jason cast a sidelong glance but tried to
appear uninterested.

"Mom, they just bought food."

"No matter, they will eat with us."

She set the cloth on a table and brought in the peanut soup in a wooden bowl and spread banana leaves on the table. Katura brought out their corn, samosas, and Fanta.

They waited while a servant girl brought Mr. Kamoga water and soap. He washed his hands while the servant girl poured water. He was a well-built man about six feet tall, lean with strong arms and hands. His hair was graying but his face was young, lit by a broad smile.

"Selina told me that you live in the lodge near the game park. I knew your father, the park ranger. Everybody around here knew him. I was on the board that passed on his selection. What a tragedy that he died." Then he bowed his head toward his food, crossed himself, and mumbled, "Excuse me for mentioning it now, but we were sad to learn of it."

He paused while the mother said a hurried grace: "We are thankful for the food and sharing it with others."

The food was tasty and satisfying to Jason. The steamed bananas and the peanut soup, the yellow-brown fried sliced cassava spiced with cinnamon, and the peppery *ntulas* were so enticing that Jason and Katura almost completely neglected the food they bought in favor of the home-cooked meal of Selina's mom. They had been so long without a home-cooked meal.

During the delicious meal, Mr. Kamoga said, "Selina also told me you were kidnapped by that crazy Lord's Liberation Army and then by poachers. As soon as we finish eating, I must know details, so I can to report it to the authorities."

Jason was surprised that Selina had in that short time explained so much to Mr. Kamoga.

He looked at Jason and Katura with admiration. "You must be quite resourceful. We don't have any record of young victims ever escaping from that murderous crew. I wish we were in the capital, where I would immediately get you an audience with the president. He has been consumed with efforts to capture that Kony, who is a thorn in the side of the three governments, Uganda, Congo, and Rwanda. All three of you are heroes! Where is the other boy, the one who escaped through the back door of the bus?"

"He's with the army unit that was camped out at my Grandpa's place in Nanansi."

"That's near where they made the big oil find."

Soon Mr. Kamoga was on the phone to the police officers and then the army who, after some minutes, located Lieutenant Ndugwa in the field. After identifying himself as a member of Parliament who held the portfolio for natural resources, Mr. Kamoga relayed all he had learned from Selina. Then he put Jason on the phone, and Jason explained how they were forced to give assistance by lending their bicycle, their stay in the poachers' camp, and its location. He described the place, the turnoff where they had spent part of the night, and the pile of burnt branches and ashes near the main road. The lieutenant knew the road that ran near the north game park, where a migratory path for animals crossed. Jason restrained his urge to ask about Biraro.

When he finished talking, Jason found their cell phone. He asked Mr. Kamoga to put the army's number in his cell phone and also his number, which the affable MP gladly did. He discovered the phone was not charged. He sent the servant girl to the shops to charge it, and Jason gave the girl twenty shillings. Mr. Kamoga did not protest, but advised the servant girl to hurry back.

Jason heard movement and voices that told him the family was large and other children were eating in an adjacent room. Peals of children's laughter came from the house next to this one.

Soon Katura was so sleepy, Jason found her nodding off. But she was polite, helping Selina do the dishes and then to spread a pallet with their blankets on the floor in the back room. Mr. Kamoga slept next door. The houses were attached and Jason heard goats bumping and bleating on the other side of the wall.

Mr. Kamoga sat outside on a bench to chat with Jason. He had worked in a service station when he was a student. He had gone to the UK where he studied business and came back as an employee of the BP oil company. He worked there until he was elected as MP and now ran his own petrol service station. He asked about Jason's plans after school.

"If my O-level scores are high enough and I get a scholarship, I'm coming back. Our government loses when students remain outside after completing studies."

"It is what is needed. I studied with a number of students who were educated by the government, but they are still abroad after many years. Three boys are in Russia, several girls are in London, and two others are studying pharmacy in America. Good jobs with overwhelming salaries are usually available to graduates. Those who study abroad are offered work even before the end of their studies. The government should have special scholarships that bind students to return home after studies abroad. I think at one time that was in force."

Jason told him about his talks with his grandmother and later with Mr. Kasamba about producing medicines here.

"I know Kasamba. He is a great herbalist. In the UK he would be a rich man, but he came back to use his education here. He is still well-off."

The servant girl brought Jason his charged telephone. She asked Katura about the gifts in her bag and the box for Grandma.

"Just two lamps," said Katura, yawning while Selina braided her hair. She noticed the girl's shawl wrapped around her waist over her skirt was familiar. The dim light prevented her from seeing the red pattern clearly.

The girl left to start the kitchen fires, and Katura gave her several matches from her backpack that she had taken from the poachers' tent when she took her parents' lamp. This servant girl was a part of Mr. Kamoga's household and slept in a house at the back of Mr. Kamoga's where there were light and electricity. The town had electricity, but his building was the only house in the village that had it.

He was enlightened like Katura's grandma and thought a light helped people to see and think. In addition to being an MP, he had an important job with the gas company in the new oil fields miles away and came home on weekends.

The girl said Mr. Kamoga had his own fuel station in the shopping center, but she had not gone during the day to get oil in her can. Since it was too late to get oil from the shops, she asked if Katura had any oil in her lamps. There was only a little oil, and the girl went her way disappointed. She would have to wait until morning.

Katura was sleeping on her pallet in Selina's room before Jason heard the mother in her room banging around. He took off his shirt and lay on his pallet. Selina put out the light and lay down between them. Drowsy, he felt her roll closer, laying her bare leg across his belly. She rolled her face very close to his lips, her warm breath flowing over his face. Now he was wide awake, her hands brushing his waist, an accidental touch while sleeping. When she did not move, he rolled away.

Then she embraced him with his blanket wrapped around his waist and legs. *Wait, this is like Father's acts in Nairobi in the darkness, now dead because of the disease there and Mother is dying, too.* Nothing can happen here. The desire's fire lit his body. His hands wanted to move over her. *No. No. No. I must not respond to her. Grandma warned me not to make rash decisions in the dark.*

Selina kept up an urgency to get him to respond. She kissed his face and murmured softly to him. There was no mistake in the way her seeking hands moved about his side, his chest, his mouth. He felt her breath, her lips.

In the darkness he whispered strongly: "No, no" to her and said: "Excuse . . . very tired . . . very tired from pedaling the bicycle all day . . ." Several more times he mumbled, for he did not want to awaken his sister or Mrs. Kamoga.

She drew away from him, quiet.

He thought about the boys at Budo Secondary School and how they talked about having sex with girls in their village. What would they think about his refusal of a lovely girl like Selina? They would laugh and ridicule his fears. *"What in the mountains were you thinking? Man, you should have buffed that one. She wanted you. And it was dark. No one would know it."*

Darkness. He did not know this village, but from his experience girls didn't go after boys. Boys went after girls this way. They might act like this out in the world, but where he lived in the sheltered game park, he didn't.

Her invitation was very dangerous, like the other threats on this journey from Munonga and the poachers. He was proud he had refused her. Selina was a beautiful girl, probably disease free, but he could not be sure.

She patted his head and whispered, "Good night, Jason. I am glad of you. You will pass high on the O-level exams. Later I will pass mine. Maybe we will meet at university."

They both drifted off to sleep. His blanket was secure around him. Once he got up and wrapped Katura's blanket tightly around her. He was glad this place was also without mosquitoes. Through the window the moon splashed a yellow sheen over the half-naked Selina, a towel wrapped around and between her legs and knotted across her stomach. He realized she had no intention of actually having sex with him. Then why did she toy with him?

Sixteen

A LOUD CRASH WOKE JASON. THEN Katura and Selina both were crawling over him, stumbling and shaking.

"Mom, what is it?" Selina cried out.

"Jason, a mountain or something exploded. People outside are screaming."

Selina's mother had a blanket wrapped around her night-clothes and stood barefooted in the doorway.

"Mom, what is it?" Selina repeated. Her mother was yelling from the doorway to Mr. Kamoga outside near the road.

Jason pulled on his trousers, shirt, and shoes and stepped out the door, shoestrings flapping. By moonlight he saw a two-tank truck lying twisted on its side across the road. It blocked the road and lay crashed into a banana plantation. Wrecked cars littered the highway. Lights flashed, horns blared disturbance. People flowed by, coming and going, yelling and arguing.

Jason saw the truck lights were still blazing as several men pulled the unresponsive driver out of the truck. "Is he dead?" someone asked. The tanks were loaded and gashes were visible on their sides. The strong acrid smell of kerosene escaping from its crushed tanks penetrated Jason's nostrils. Many covered their faces.

A crowd of jabbering half-dressed people collected in the road, pointing and yelling information about the crash. A line was forming; some ran toward the crash with calabashes and shiny five-gallon cans to fill with the kerosene that spurted in silver, gurgling leaks from several broken places in the wrecked tanker.

Mr. Kamoga darted up and down the road halting cars that tried to detour around the truck into the banana *shamba*. "Danger!" he shouted again and again. "Very dangerous! You will die!" He repeated the warning again and again. Several people yelled back, drowning out his insistent voice with accusations.

"He owns a petrol station and works for the company. Don't you want to have free petrol?" said one man.

"They steal from you. Now is our chance to steal the kerosene."

"Don't listen. He's an MP with the government."

"Don't listen. He is with the owners, the exploiters," several men shouted. They ran to get containers. Soon the road was lined with people filling their cans.

The truck lights were turned off, ordered by Mr. Kamoga. "If there is a spark, people will die."

Still, no one listened and more people came. The road was jammed all the way up to the shops on the curving hill as people jostled and contended for a place in line. Jason, Katura, and Mrs. Kamoga watched, while Selina ran back and forth to the house to look after the little children.

Mr. Kamoga went to the middle of the road and talked to people in line. They listened, but no one left their place in line.

Jason and Katura and Selina went closer to see the wreck. They stood in the road, watching people fill their large five-gallon containers with the fuel. Except for moonlight, it was dark and the kerosene scent was very strong. It splashed on the clothing of people carrying cans. Although they were drenched with the liquid and odor, they filled more cans and hurried away.

Jason saw the several leaks gushing kerosene where a line of people with large fuel cans, gourds, or bottles in hand or on their shoulders waited their turn. He listened to Mr. Kamoga tirelessly yelling and trying to warn everyone away. The more he begged and shouted, the more people came. He finally threw up his hands in disappointment; it was no use. He came back to Selina's mother and said, "It won't be long, now. This can't last. Someone will do something stupid and it will all be over."

Selina's mother was very upset that no one listened to him. Finally, she waved to the children to follow her back to the house, looking at the sky. "It's almost dawn."

Mr. Kamoga shook his head, followed her, and ordered the servants to run the goats to the uphill pasture.

Then the servant girl with a lamp started across the road. "I'll help people see to get the kerosene faster." She stopped near the cab of the tanker.

Katura touched Jason's arm. "Look, that's our lamp that we took back from the poachers. She's got our lamp. I gave her matches."

"She is a good girl. She must be going to fill it with oil for you," said Selina's mother. "She must return quickly or Mr. Kamoga will be upset with her."

With the mention of matches and the lamp, Jason suddenly remembered a flash of the scene he witnessed in the poachers' camp. Abdul poured gasoline on a rag and tossed it on a pile of trash. He lit his cigarette, threw the match, and the whole pile caught on fire.

Whooom!

He also remembered the surprised look on Abdul's face, alarmed, as he beat out the flames burning a bush. At that moment Jason knew what Mr. Kamoga was trying to tell the crowd: the danger of a violent gas explosion.

What Mr. Kamoga was saying was true! If anyone there lighted a match or smoked a cigarette near the torn tanker, it would be a death trap for all.

"Listen to Mr. Kamoga, all of you!! He's right" he cried out. He caught one man's arm, "Sir, if all of you don't leave now, you are going to die." He looked in the man's face. He stormed through the crowd, pulling people out of line. "Danger! You must get away!"

They shrugged him off, pushed him aside, and accused him of breaking line. One began hitting and pummeling him, knocking him to the ground. Jason threw up his hand, held his head, and touched his lips—his mouth was bleeding.

Selina and Katura helped him up. Then he shook himself, "It's no use, nobody listens. The kerosene is driving them mad."

He took the girls' arms and scrambled back toward the house. "Everybody is crazy. We must get our bicycle and things. We must leave this place or we will die with them."

By the time Jason got his bicycle and Katura had her backpack and blanket, Mr. Kamoga had gathered his family in the back of Selina's mother's house. Jason gripped the handlebars, tasting his blood on his lips, the first light of day shining over the hills. His voice though quiet and firm held an edge of urgency when he said, "It is time to go. Mr. Kamoga is a man of experience and he says all of this is dangerous. I, too, believe him. It is hopeless. We cannot save anyone, but we must save ourselves. Let's hurry." He started down the road beside the wrecked truck.

"But you can't go that way," cried Mrs. Kamoga from the side of the house with her husband and children. "You'll never make it through that crowd. The road is blocked . . . everything is blocked! They are waiting, not moving aside for anyone. It is like they are wild. Go through the fields in back of our house." She pointed the way. "This small path gets wider as you go along. It meets the main road further on."

They joined the family and ran through the banana and cassava plantations. They hurried down footpaths and bicycle trails. People passed them carrying cans of kerosene on their shoulders, disappearing into houses. Jason heard their running feet on the path and their heavy breathing as they ran by him.

Katura poked him in the ribs and said, "Jason, Jason, look there, on the road below."

She pointed to two Land Rovers that had drawn up to the cab beside the wrecked tanker truck.

"It's the poachers. They must have been chasing us." One climbed up on the door to search the empty cab.

Jason and Katura ran ahead, not looking back. After they climbed along farms of fruit trees to the crest of the hill, Mr. Kamoga pointed down far below. Several small lights glittered now and then. "Do you see that? Some fools are smoking cigarettes."

Jason nodded. "Yes, sir. If someone lights a match the whole tanker will blow up."

Mr. Kamoga nodded. "And everything around it. Wherever there is kerosene, the fire will race. If our houses remain, they will be terribly damaged. But, oh, the number of dead or injured, you can't imagine." He shook his head. "These are the people who voted for me. It is very sad."

His wife caught his hand and said, "Let us hope it doesn't happen. You tried, but no one would listen."

Jason was close to him. "Many will die?"

"Those who do not die will be burned and disfigured with the skin all hanging about them, sick from now until they die. That's what happens when oil is dug from the ground among ignorant people who do not know its power and explosive quality. They have had no experience, no opportunity to be educated.

"Our people have never experienced anything like it, so they could not know. I have seen the same thing at a petrol station in Europe. Someone lit a cigarette. There was an explosion that rocked the station and killed a dozen people. That was nothing compared to this. In that small city in England, there were hospitals and ambulances around. People were treated at once. Here, there will be hundreds. And we have only that one-man dispensary up the hill on the road in Rendutu village. Wherever they have spilled kerosene in the bush, even in their houses where the cans are. There will be a trail for the flash of fire. It will go there like magic."

Mr. Kamoga's voice went on lamenting like a chant. "It happened in Nigeria when people broke the oil line that ran through the jungle in an effort to get fuel. Someone lit a match and a village died. In the Congo, it happened the same way. Now this truck comes from the refinery near our new oil wells."

Now from their hillside they heard a voice crying out: "*Kiberite!* Who has a *kiberite?* I can't see."

"They are yelling for matches," Mrs. Kamoga shouted.

"If someone supplies one, it is all over."

A sudden warning flash was followed by flashes down there and up the hillside. Then a humming grew to a soft roar and a loud *Vroom!* Banana trees were blown backwards. Debris, branches, and parts of houses flew past Jason. His eyes stung and his mouth was dry and bitter.

Everything was blurred, but Jason saw the area around the tanker was blazing. The long, heartbreaking screams frightened him.

Mr. Kamoga turned to Jason. "Go on now. This path will take you across the curve to the highway."

"Mother, give me one of my brothers and let me accompany them to where the path meets the main road," said Selina. Katura put her arms around her.

And Jason thought of Selina's seeking arms and lips during the night. To him she was just a girl student in Senior-4. He was waiting for his O-level results and would go to college. He was proud of his strength and how he had resisted during the night. It had turned out best for both of them. But why was she so eager to go and show them the way?

Mrs. Kamoga readily agreed. She picked Juma, one of Selina's young brothers, who seemed strong and sturdy. In Primary-4, he smiled, carrying a smooth stick.

The four of them set out along the path that went loping into the hills. They soon lost sight of the crowd on the hillside with Mr. Kamoga, but in the valley on the roadway below, the tanker blazed and muffled screams of agony reached them.

SEVENTEEN

THEY HIKED TO THE CREST of the hillside where the path widened into a road. Breaking daylight revealed terraced gardens of potatoes, peanuts, and cassava replacing bananas and pineapple. Wild flowers in bloom scented the humid air and insects hummed. Selina, walking beside Katura, laughed.

"For the longest time, Mr. Kamoga tells Mom, people didn't live up here because they thought it was too close to God. That was a strange thing for them to say. Our family came from a small village south of here, near a place of cows. Oh, you've never seen so many cows. I go there often to visit my cousin."

Katura said, "After last night some of them probably remembered how from down there the clouds seemed to cover this place. They probably are in Heaven."

"Well, they call it the Sky High Road and I just love it up here. When I finish my studies, I would come back here to live."

Jason said, "You mean you came from Mbuzi. That is near the place where that Liberation Army kidnapped us."

"Oh yes," she said, "we have family there. In fact I will be visiting them in a week's time."

Jason was distracted by the pungent scent of orange and lemon trees in bloom along the roadside. Looking more closely, he saw many of the leaves and branches covered with humming and buzzing yellow bees. He walked closer to the girls waiting for Selina to tell more about her home village.

Silver beads of dew hung from the yellow nipples of lemons, sparkling in the early morning light. Trees stood silent and composed in the windless morning. The bicycle tires crunched gravel as they rolled along in answer to the gritting sound of the soles of the heavy shoes Jason wore. His father's shoes were always a point of pride with him.

Selina and Katura chatted while Jason listened in secret.

The hot yellow sunlight nudged away the night's fog. They looked down into the valley on the road where the tanker had exploded. Now it was too far away to make out individual people moving down there. If people still moved down there. It had been blazing hell with screams, exploding cars, and loud curses with people moving up and down.

Birds in the trees sang, cattle on the sides of the hill grazed, cows frolicked and skittered, their mouths grabbing at branches and any green growth about them in the high grass. Bees flew up around them. Children played in front of their houses. Juma chased children on and off the path.

The bowl of blue sky hung with white puffy clouds just above Jason, almost within reach. The faraway sounds echoed from the roadway below. It seemed that they had escaped from the hell below and now were laughing and talking in the clouds.

He had noticed that Selina was usually a quiet young woman. Now he thought the girl talked loudly, as if she wanted him to hear. Though she was nearer to Katura, she was actually talking to him. When he came near them rolling the bicycle, she was talking about her favorite books—Jomo Kenyata's *Facing*

Mount Kenya, Tom Brown's *School Days, The Life of a Luo Girl,* and those by Jane Austen.

"My oldest sister is married and lives in Masaka. When my mother announced the wedding, I was so surprised. I thought Aretha had gone out of her mind because neither of us ever cared for the company of boys. Now she was going to live with one? I felt she was a stranger to me. Does Jason read a lot?"

Katura nodded. Selina said that would increase his scores on O-levels.

Katura said, "I see even in the hurry to leave your house last night you still brought away school things in your backpack."

"That's for sure. I have my books right here. But about my sister, I felt deceived. I felt my whole family had deceived me, you know, left me out of things. Both my mother and grandmother said it is very dangerous now to cultivate any kind of association with members of the opposite sex because of AIDS."

"Yes, but there are others," said Katura.

"I would be glad to hear the reasons, because everyone is concerned. Men have to be better known before marriage."

Jason wanted to hear more, but the girls' voices dropped to whispers as they lagged farther behind.

Selina pointed. "Look, bees are everywhere, on plant leaves and zooming through the air. Uncle Lev Lugazi studies bees and sells honey, and he said whenever we burn grasses and trees it disturbs their work in the hives and the plants. Many will rush away in swarms. He used to be a park ranger but quit because of danger from the poachers. And the government did nothing to stop them."

Jason bent down to remove a leafy branch caught in the metal spokes of the bicycle tire, glanced back, and studied the girl. She was tall and shapely; her face was handsome with a medium-sized mouth and little pouting lips. Her hair was carefully combed. Even though they had all dressed hurriedly, she had chosen her clothes wisely on the spot and taken care to wash her face. The black-and-white patterned skirt accented her slim figure, and her blouse emphasized ample breasts. He remembered the naked girl on the floor in the moonlight from the previous night. Her actions didn't match the schoolgirl now on the trail. He recalled her neat home, her mother's charm, and her father's understanding manner.

"Which side of the ferry do you live on?" asked Selina.

"We live next to the game park," said Katura.

"So Jason goes to Kisubi Secondary. Oh, you must know my cousins, the Ochingos, my uncle's family."

Jason stopped the bicycle and stared at her. Katura hugged her. "Then you're cousins to Mbabazi and Biraro?"

This surprised and shocked Jason. Why was Katura hugging her just because she was a cousin to Mbabazi, when Katura barely had ever heard of Mbabazi before this trip?

"Selina, Biraro is our special friend."

Jason winced. Biraro was now close to his sister. He wanted to pursue the topic but thought it best not to appear too interested.

"I missed one year of school because of the measles," said Selina. Jason calculated that she was in Senior-4, like she had said back in the market.

"Now, Katura, what about boys' habits? What if they had good character and did not drink and go to the bars? Hard to know. My sister found a way to know her husband better."

Katura stopped on the path, "How did she do that? I loved Father but that was one of his failings. He spent time at bars drinking and meeting strange people. Mother never knew until after they were married. In the end it killed him. And that's the cause of Mother's illness now."

"Knowing their behavior is very important, and girls have to find out before they marry. My sister went to extremes to know it."

"I don't see how she could find out."

Jason didn't understand what Selina was getting at in the vague questions. His attention was taken by the little brother, Juma, who swung from the limb of a nearby tree and dropped onto the seat of the bicycle. Before that, he'd walked alongside him most of the time. From the beginning he had vied for Jason's attention by disappearing from the road, hiding among the trees and bushes and vines on the roadside, then reappearing again. He even once hung upside down from a limb of a tree across the road and released himself, dropping down, laughing at the startled Jason.

"What do you think you're doing, Juma?"

He answered, throwing his arms up and down and smiling with wry humor. "Proving you don't know."

"Don't know what? "

"Whatever you want to know but don't know how to know it. Even if you have finished Senior-4."

"Why don't I know what?"

"My sister is in Senior-4, and she has to teach you what I already know."

"She is teaching me? What?"

"She says she will pass O-levels because she reads everything, everywhere. You passed last night, but will you pass O-levels?" He laughed and ran away up a tree that arched up and threw shade across the road, and soon he sat in the grass near the road on the opposite side, waiting.

"What should I read? What books?"

"There are many. Some Father brings home. Things she reads like you would like to know but won't ask her. Mother and my married sister brought her a very old book. She taught you all last night. She likes tests."

"Look, Juma, I know things. I see things and think them through."

Jason was talking to him when the boy suddenly disappeared behind a tree and reappeared in a growth among someone's garden plants along the way. "If you don't see, you may think you know, but you don't. Do you know what they are saying?" He nodded and pointed with his nose at the girls.

"It's just girl talk."

"No. It is about you. When I'm behind or near them hanging above as they pass I heard talk of you last night. She thinks you're a good man."

"Did she tell my sister that?" Jason was surprised and embarrassed.

"She just said you passed the test."

Juma plopped a much used, coverless book into Jason's hands. When they stopped to rest Jason hid behind a bush and opened the book. The index was there, and so he looked to find tribal coming-of-age customs. He had read this book before and vaguely remembered it. He found the section where young coming-of-age men and women slept in the same quarters but girls were respected and not forced to do sex. The girls bound their legs and sex organs with towels so disrespectful boys would not be successful. They would be reported to all of the girls. They would have a hard time finding a mate.

Wow! Now he understood Selina's actions. Girls tested boys to see if they were irresponsible and would have sex with anyone. It was a test to protect women from AIDS. Some boys would be just like his father who brought disease home. Selina had tested him.

Jason came out from behind the bush. Juma was rolling an orange in his hands, laughing and looking sly. He hid the orange behind him, brought it out like a magician, and held it firmly in front of him, put his thumbs in it, and popped it open.

"Look, now you see!" Then quickly he took it away. "Now Selina makes me practice with her. How many parts?"

Jason stared. "Eh, four. Or is it six?"

Then Juma pulled a flower with petals from behind his back—"How many petals?"—and hid it quickly.

No time, you must answer quickly. Jason was familiar with these tests; they ran them on each other at school. It was clear that Selina was in the hard study group that every good school had. He approved of Selina and her brother, but she had deceived him. What if he had been weak enough to do what she suggested?

He handed the book to Juma. Then he took an orange, kicked it high, and kept it in the air, alternating kicks with feet and head bumps. Juma was fascinated with his rhythm. His eyes got big and followed the movement of the fruit as Jason kept tapping it.

"Get ready. It's coming your way!"

Juma was not ready. The orange bobbed and skirted away in the grass. "Amazed I failed that test. How do you do that?"

"Another kind of practice! You are a very clever eight-year-old."

"No! My mother and sister are testing us every day. Sometimes we all fail."

When they stopped for rest, Jason handed the bicycle over to the girls and walked with Juma. The boy twisted a supple branch stripped of leaves and twigs into a circle. Again he ran in and out among trees and branches, disappearing and appearing in different places along the way in the most entertaining way.

Selina struck up a short rhythmic tune, clapping her hands in a way that inspired Juma's movements. It was practiced and one could tell that it was something done at family gathering. He knew which bark would peel off in strips from a branch, and he expertly removed this skin intact, whirling it around his circle and tying it. Suddenly Juma had made a small wheel without spokes. Then he found a forked stick along the trail and set his wheel in motion, rolling it forward on the ground, sending it forward and back and to the side, steering with his stick.

"Please, can you help me make one like that?" asked Jason. So they found two like branches, and soon the both of them had their wheeled devices running in and out between the two girls and the bicycle and other people on the road, who laughed at their antics.

"It must be fun to have a big brother," said Selina.

"Well, maybe, sometimes," said Juma, laughing and bumping into her.

She stuck out her foot to trip him as he came by her with his wheel. He avoided her cleanly and from behind his back gave her a *whomp*, a playful tap on her backside with his steering stick.

Both girls laughed. "Oh," said Katura, after he swatted her. "Here, Jason, take your old bicycle. I'm tired."

As the sun rose higher, the landscape was flatter, and the grass and bush taller. Instead of farms, herds of massive horned cattle came up near the roadway since there were no fences.

Jason was all smiles here. This brought memories of his father before they moved to the park lodge. He had loved cows as a small boy when they lived on Grandpa's land.

Some shops appeared along the way. Jason counted his money, remembering he had not paid Selina's mother for the night's lodging.

"Everything was so scary last night, you must forgive us," Katura said, embarrassed.

Selina was surprised. "We never thought of it. Besides you did not sleep the whole night. Mother won't care if we never collect." But Jason insisted she take two shillings before he could spend any money. Juma left them to play with some children near the road. Jason praised the boy's friendly personality.

"Oh, we already know these people. They are Mom's family, they live near here. In fact some of these cows we have seen are theirs. We visit here often. That's why Mom and Father didn't mind us coming away here after that disaster with the tanker," Selina said.

She further persuaded them not to spend money. "We should have tea with my Uncle Lev Lugazi, the honey peddler." She pointed to a house some distance from the roadway and led the way. Juma and other young girls and boys crowded around Selina, pulling at her skirt and holding her hands. At the side of the house, many empty gourds of various sizes were stacked on a low table. Inside, several women of different ages welcomed them. Then a man came in who looked familiar to Jason. He greeted them and asked where they were going. They told him, and he asked if they were of the family of Rendutu. "My father is Peter," Jason said.

Lugazi's face split in a wide grin, showing his big white teeth. "Like your father, I am also a former game ranger."

Selina's aunt served tea with honey, bread, and milk. They ate and rested, sitting under papaya trees near the house. Lev Lugazi said he would be in Mbuzi in two days with a load of honey. Then he said, "You know, your father comes from some-where in the hills." He pointed with his nose. "Your grandpa, the father of your mother, was a Saza chief and had many cows."

Jason remembered poems read in school that described the magnetic rhythms of the herders' dances. He had learned them as a child when he was among them with his mother and father. He was a herder by birth although he lived in an alien place, the game park with a high metal fence separating his family from the animals. They might as well be inmates, fellows of the animals in a city zoo.

He felt now a great urge to go out among the herdsmen. They were now very near the main road where he and Katura should continue their way home to Grandma and take to her that precious lamp. But when would he get the chance to visit these animals again? His father had gone to school, learned to be a game ranger, and cut all ties with that past life while the family still kept it alive.

Jason left Katura with Selina and went out to seek the herd boys, accompanied by Juma and his cousins and nieces and nephews. Jason joined the circle of dancers and imitated their movement with the staff held out as a spear to protect the herd. They danced and leapt, and the music carried to the house, so soon everyone came out to watch. It seemed that Jason had known this before, because he did not have to learn the steps and the leaps. When music stopped, he threw down his staff, thrilled.

Jason tried not to show his sadness as they left. He avoided Katura's tear-filled eyes. Instead he became very busy and concerned with getting the bicycle ready—tying on backpacks, checking the pressure in the tires—doing anything that kept him from engaging anyone closely.

When they were set to go, Lugazi came out and told them the highway was less than a mile away. Selina refused to part from them until they reached it. By this time, she and Katura had become such fast friends that parting was difficult.

A crowd of young people walked the mile or more to the place where the Sky High Road joined the regular highway. The girls were busy exchanging information, telling each other what schools they attended and describing the very road to their schools and the distances, promising they would soon meet again. Selina's cousin, Mbabazi, lived very near and was at this moment living with Grandmother in their house. With many tears, handclasps, and hugs, they parted.

Juma was very sad and not playful. He followed Jason even after they had boarded their bicycle. He ran alongside, waving, jumping, and singing. Earlier, he tried to give Jason his wheel to take with him. But Selina took him aside and explained Jason wanted it but could not take it with him on the bicycle, for they had far to travel.

They stood by the road, a dozen people from the Sky High Road village, and waved until the tearful Katura, looking back, could no longer see them. They rode along in silence, listening to the tweak and hum of the tires of the bicycle against the roadway.

"Jason, didn't you like her?"

Jason pedaled faster, putting more force in the downward thrust of his legs, pumping, concentrating. He did not answer. He craned his neck as if he searched the roadway ahead for something.

"Jason, I know you heard me. Did you like my friend, Selina?" She held him tighter by the waist for support. He pedaled rapidly.

"I guess so. She was all right, I guess."

Katura pinched his side hard. "Ah! Be truthful, Jason. You know you liked her."

Both of them laughed. The bicycle sped on.

EIGHTEEN

THE ROAD TO THE RUIZI River rolled like a black ribbon between the green hills. Jason was disturbed. There were no signs to point the way.

His legs were lead. He was fast coming to his limit. Katura was tired also. He felt the looseness of her arms as she slumped around his middle. Was she asleep? He needed her support as he pedaled madly, forcing the bicycle on.

Her voice was listless, but she would never plead tiredness. Women taught their daughters to be tireless workers beside their husbands. He had once heard his mother talking to Katura when she had walked a long way carrying food bags from the ferry. *"Don't just slump about like you are dying. Use your energy. You will drop a bag and spill something. There is plenty of time to rest later. Keep moving."* Katura had continued, struggling with the big bags, and finally brought them inside.

Now as they walked uphill and coasted down, papyrus fronds twisted in the breezes like a mad farmer's crop. A bog sank in the middle of the road where furry cattails and purple thistles showered cottony seed parachutes into sultry air. Boys on the hillside with a herd of cows played flutes. Another listened to a radio, the BBC news in Australia.

"Tired, Jason?"

He was breathing fast in the wind with no energy to answer.

Cardinals sporting their red feathers and yellow weavers flew up from the bushes and perched on a papyrus's fan-shaped leaves bobbing under their weight. "No signs on the road," he huffed. "Nothing to guide us."

"But, Jason, there is one," she said raising one arm from his waist to point.

"Where? I haven't seen a single one."

"I have seen many signs. Some are half hidden by growth on the roadside. You have become a work zebra. You've been so busy pedaling and looking for big colorful signs that tell you where to eat or the yellow ones for Fanta or to buy Bata shoes. See, there's one."

He pulled the bicycle up to it and slumped near a small bush in its shade. It was a disappointment—a block of concrete with its top slightly pointed. It reminded Jason of grave markers he'd seen in cemeteries. They had recently seen many, no wonder he had not noticed. His mind rejected something that told him someone was buried at that spot, but here on the roadway such a sign or marker told a different story in heartbreaking symbols. Jason could not believe it. What did it mean, MILE above a 22?

"Meaning what?" He looked at her from where he rested beside the sign.

As tired as she was, she smiled at him. "Poor Jason, I have never seen you when you couldn't think straight . . . Ha, ha, ha."

"What do you mean? I am only tired. Who says I can't think straight? Look at you, dragging along. Do you deny that you're tired?"

"Well, yes, I'm tired! We both are tired. You're like, well, like you're grieving or something . . . worse."

"You mean, I am grieving over a road sign? That makes no sense."

"Right, I am tired and very hungry. To me, the sign makes sense."

"So what? Tell me then, Miss Teacher, Katura, woman of the world."

Her shoulders raised, her eyes widened, and she looked prettily around and up in the sky.

"It says what it means. We are twenty-two miles from somewhere."

"And, well, Miss, what is that somewhere and how do you decide that it is what you say it is?" He sounded like his science teacher, Mr. Eru.

"Well, if you were down here on the road, with your passenger instead of Mr. Proud up on his pedals, racing the world and pretending . . . just pretending, you would know what the sign says."

With a little rest Jason's mind was clearing. What was she saying now? What was this new thing . . . pretending? He thought he got it . . . but wait . . .

"OK, OK. Just tell me what the sign says first."

"What do you mean, first?"

"Katura," he pointed, three of his fingers in the air, and waved them before her. "You're being devious. Tell me about the sign."

"Well, the MILE 22 means we have come twenty-two miles from somewhere or we have twenty-two miles to go to get to somewhere."

"And so?" He sounded a bit like his geometry teacher. "Go on."

"I have been watching these signs for a long time. If we'd been talking I would have told you . . . reminded you, you know . . ."

"Why are you stopping?"

"Well, the first one I saw after we left that high village and came onto this road said MILE 64 and they have been getting smaller since then and now MILE 22 means we have come 42 miles and have 22 miles to go to get to Ruizi town."

He looked at her in amazement. "Katura, this trip has done a lot for both of us, but I am amazed at you." He hugged her briefly and said, "Now you're so smart, pedal this bicycle those twenty-two miles."

"Jason, I am too hungry."

"Not too hungry to explain how I am proud and pretending, I hope. Because you will not eat a mouthful of anything until you explain what you meant."

"Well, there's not any place to eat, and there's no money to buy."

"Well, you'd better think up what you'll say when we get food 'cause I'll torture you until you tell me what you meant."

"I don't remember what you're talking about. What are you doing with that?"

Jason was opening a little metal kit clamped to the bicycle frame. "Oh, this holds the patching for a tire. If you get a puncture." He struggled to loosen the flap but it was rusted to the body of the kit. "You see, Katura, if we had a coin, we could pry this open."

She looked at him and laughed. "If we had a coin, we wouldn't be searching for one in that old rusted thing."

"Go ahead and laugh. We'll see how funny it is when I'm eating a roasted ear of corn or baked cassava."

"Jason, please don't do that." Her hands folded in prayer. Her stomach growled with hunger.

"Do what?" he asked innocently. "Ouch!" He broke a fingernail on the rusted tin.

"Please don't mention the name of a food. I'll die of hunger if you do."

"Ah!" The tin opened but there was only a rubber patch, a tube of rubber paste, and a little rough serrated metal strip for cleaning the tire before putting on the patch. "Well, we can't eat that." Disgusted, he closed the rusted tin and banged it back in place on the bicycle frame. "We better try to eat up that twenty-two miles," he said, looking under the seat and along the frame. There was the useless bicycle pump and the flashlight held onto the frame with a metal clamp.

"Hey, I wonder." He said, unloosening the clamp that held the flashlight in place.

"You wonder what?"

"You know Grandpa said it wouldn't work, he had tried it. Besides, who could eat an old useless flashlight? You know," he went on talking to himself, "when batteries get bad, they sometimes put a copper coin in back to help the battery light up. Maybe there is one here. Let's see." He twisted the end that held the batteries. "It's rusted together, too."

"Well, you ought to hit it on the ground like we hit a jar top on a table if it won't open."

Jason hit it the flashlight on the ground several times, then turned it, twisted back and forth, and then with difficulty twisted it, with his tongue poking out of the side of his mouth. After great effort, it clanked open with an unexpected clanking sound. It didn't hold a dead flashlight battery after all.

Money fell out. Shilling coins. A few copper pence coins. And paper money: a folded, wrinkled five-shilling note.

"Hey, hey, Katura, Grandpa never rode this bike at night so he stored his change here when he went to the market during the day."

"Well, we can eat now."

"Impossible." Jason shook his head.

"What? Don't talk crazy. I'm hungry. Let's go until we find a market and buy food."

She lifted the bicycle onto its wheels, ready to go.

He shook his head sadly, while getting on the bicycle, "You see, we can't spend the money. We don't have Grandpa's permission."

Katura looked at Jason as if he had lost his mind.

He put the money in his pocket, laughing. "We have to take this money to Grandma. It is her husband's money. We can't spend it."

"You're one crazy brother. You'll never make it home. I'll do you in before you get there." They were back on the bicycle laughing, and she was slapping his head and face.

"We still can't eat, or at least you can't, until you explain all of your irrational accusations."

"Go faster, Jason," she laughed.

At mile MILE 20 they came upon a group of shops by the road, and the peddlers came out with roasting corn, baked potatoes, slices of roasted nuts, platters of cassava, baked chicken, strips of roasted goat, cheeses, and bread and bottles of orange and lemon Fanta. Jason placed the bicycle under a low mvule tree.

Katura beckoned him over where she was choosing foods. "Please pay two-and-a-half shillings." She had the food and was already popping roasted groundnuts into her mouth.

Katura spread out their blankets. He was chewing on cassava and drinking a lemon soda. "We're not leaving this spot until you tell me what you meant." He held her soda away from her.

"I need my drink. Do you want me to choke?" She faked choking while chewing.

"Pretending? What did you mean by that?" He waved the drink in her direction. As she reached for it, he yanked it back again.

"Gimme, I'll tell you true." He gave her the soda. After she gulped, she said, "Yes, I remember we had just started out and you were pretending it didn't matter that you were leaving every-one back on that Sky High Road. You were on the bike pedaling and not looking back. You were sickening, phony, and fake. It was a shame how you left Selina, my friend."

She took another swallow of her drink and went on. "When I asked you if you liked her, could you be honest about it? After all, we were alone then. Well, you didn't even answer until I begged you. And what did you say? 'I guess she's all right.' You know you liked her a lot. You were just too proud to say it—even to me." She pointed to her chest with the thumb of the hand holding the roasted ear of corn.

Jason was quiet for a long while. Finally, he said, "There's something about the night we slept there at their house that you don't know."

"If there's something you know about my friend, you can tell me."

"Not now, I'm too tired. There's no way I can pedal another twenty miles. We need to ride the bus."

"Again? Remember what happened the last time we took a bus?"

"Yes, Grandpa said that the Liberation Army had been chased back to the Sudan. They are no longer about here."

"Then if it's safe, let's go by bus."

"What about your hair? One side is tightly plaited and the other side is loose."

"Yes, I can fix that. Selina fixed only one side last night. I just need a few minutes." She began fumbling with her hair. "I don't have my comb, but . . ." She ran her fingers through her hair, gathering it to plait it.

"No, I was wondering if you had any money left there in those plaits before we spend money on bus fare."

"I had forgotten. When we were hungry we should have thought about it." She felt in her hair. "No money there now. We used it all long ago."

"Then we can only ride as far as that bridge and pay a shilling each. Then we must walk and ride the bicycle to the ferry, which is about ten miles further."

They wrapped up their food and got the bicycle ready to put on the bus. They felt safe with all of the people around, buying food and talking.

"Jason, please tell me about Selina while we wait."

"Not now, but I promise to tell you later. You're right though, I do like her."

Katura's eyes sparkled. "I knew it . . . and no matter what you think, she's good." They rested in the shade until the bus horn awakened them. Jason put the bicycle up on the rack, and they took seats side by side and went to sleep. Neither of them awoke until Katura was given a baby to mind, dozing again with the baby on her lap.

After sunset, the bus arrived at the bridge. Jason had planned for them to sleep in the town, but there was a crowd of people waiting in the road and on the hillside above the bridge. They took down the bicycle and joined them.

A man approached, "I don't think your bus will cross here tonight. The bees aren't letting anyone cross."

NINETEEN

THE ROAD CURVED AROUND A HILL at the four-way stop. The Catholic mission cathedral and school were uphill on the right. Straight ahead was the highway going toward Tanzania and to the left was the roadway across the bridge into Ruizi town. Traffic moved along the road above the bridge, but no one turned and crossed the bridge. Vehicles were parked on the road in front of the mission entry or farther down on the road to the bridge. Jason pushed the bicycle away from the bus to the top of the hill, then alongside the crowd of people blocking the road. More and more people came and filled the space behind them.

Jason's legs felt loose, strong, and ready. He was no longer tired or achy but that felt after a night's sleep he could pedal the bicycle home. Beside him, Katura breathed deeply of the air outside the bus. She gripped the bag that held their grandmother's lamp.

A large crowd of people blocked the road and the hillside leading down to the bridge. They were looking down the roadway toward the bridge, but nobody moved in that direction.

"Why are we stopping here?" Katura whispered. She had not whispered to him before, and he did not know why she did it now. He caught snatches of the words people were shouting near them—"Honey," and "Bees."

They peered above the heads of the crowd, down where they stood on the road and to the river below. Jason was not disturbed by the talk of bees. He remembered what Selina said about them moving when they were disturbed by the grass fires started by the tanker truck explosion. Could they have travel forty or fifty miles?

The road to the river was hard gray tarmac with large potholes where big trucks had scarred it. On the opposite side near Ruizi, Jason saw four or five people gathered, waiting to cross back. He heard "Bees" and "Swarm" and "Taking their honey."

The bridge was clear. He did not understand why so many people were blocking the road. They were standing near bicycles, a bus, and a line of cars. They all blocked the way, but no one attempted to cross the bridge. If the crowd would just move aside and stop blocking the road, Jason could pedal fast with Katura on the carriage seat. They would speed past the people with bundles on their heads and schoolboys with small herds of goats waiting to go down to the river to drink on the other side. And they would race into Ruizi.

Near him a man in short pants and no shirt was saying the same thing. He was chewing a wad of brown tobacco leaves and intermittently spitting out a splash of brown liquid from his mouth onto green tree leaves covering the ground. He waved his thin arm and empty hand as though it was a wand or a baton, directing people to flow across. "It's clear. Just go fast. They can't get out."

"What are you talking about?" Jason asked.

A short man with the wizened beard said, "That's crazy. They would never make it across. The bees will get them."

Another man in a faded blue hospital jacket said, "And if you're allergic to the stings, you could die."

"Where are the bees?" Jason asked. "I don't see any bees." Then he heard the droning and felt the swarm whip by his head. Several people in the crowd slapped at their heads and clothing.

"I don't see any bees," said Katura.

The old man came near to the bicycle, gently took her hand, and pointed. "Look above on the bridge girders. You see that, there, what looks like a huge brown bag or cloud? That's where they are—the bees. That's a swarm and nobody will get through."

"But it is high. How will it stop people from walking across?" said Jason.

"There are many soldier bees flying down low near us, guarding the bridge and the swarm," the jacketed man explained.

Jason didn't intend to wait here all night with this crowd, packed and immobile.

A voice behind Jason shouted, "Move aside. Let me through!"

At first nobody heeded the insistent voice. Nobody gave an inch. The packed crowd of people turned to stare but refused to move. They were pushed and pummeled from behind. A man with a loaded bicycle was forcing his way through the crowd. "Move aside. Let me pass."

Jason pushed their bicycle farther away up the side of the hill so he could see down into the crowd. He wanted to see the intruder more clearly. He was a brown-skinned, muscular man with alert eyes and a demanding voice that boomed through the crowd. It was Lev Lugazi, whom they had met on the Sky High Road.

"Is he going to the market again with honey? Where does he get it all? He robs from the bees and sells their honey. It's Lugazi from Chalo!" said the tall man.

A gourd, wide as a barrel and as high as the man's head, was strapped on the bicycle's carriage seat. At the top of the curved neck, a thick braid of grass sealed the opening. As the man passed through the crowd, the gourd gave off a sweet odor. A woman cried out, "Ah, *bom, bay! Bom, bay!* If he is allowed to go there and disturb that swarm, nobody will cross this bridge for days. Somebody reason with him."

Several men grabbed the handlebars and stopped the honey peddler's progress.

Jason saw his chance to cross the bridge. He rolled his bicycle up the ridge above the road. Suddenly the rumbling of vehicles and the blaring of horns rose from the highway coming from Bukoba, Tanzania. Gunshots rang out, followed by the zoom of two fast-approaching vehicles in a whirl of brown dust.

The crowd split in the roadway as the battered blue van with windows down skidded to a stop. A tall man wielded a stick out of the window, striking those blocking the way. He yelled, "Make way, damn you!"

A boy poked a rifle through the side windows and fired several times. An old woman and two men lay in the road bleeding. The small driver, his right hand on the steering wheel and the left waving a handgun, fired again and again.

Jason recognized his captors—Tempo the Pygmy, Rufu, and the commander Munonga. They had escaped capture by the government army and now intended to cross the bridge. Tempo gunned the motor and the van skidded from side to side, aiming for the roadway to the bridge. He missed it.

Lugazi's bicycle with the gourd of honey was resting on the roadway above the bridge when a second van appeared. The skilled driver, coming at a terrific speed, overshot the road, but corrected the error by braking and skidding, turning almost around, slinging the vehicle's rear end so that it crashed into Lugazi's bicycle.

With a loud *"Plommp! Screech!"* the gourd was smashed to smithereens.

The little agile driver of this van was Yuri, another of Munonga's men. Looking from side to side in front and behind him all at once, after grinding the gears and twisting and turning the steering wheel, he straightened the van and took off at full speed across the bridge. A spiral of bees chased, but the van crossed the bridge.

Yuri quickly parked on the uphill grade past the bridge, jumped out, and grabbed branches to beat about the car. Several little women jumped out from the back and did the same motions. Then the car took off on the road above the town going full speed.

The shooting and chaos had aroused the swarm of bees into activity, engulfing the first van while it idled on the bank.

"Rufu, for the Lord's Liberation Army, you bloody well shoot anyone who moves. Tempo, cross the damn bridge now! Pay attention! Do your job," ordered Munonga.

The motor revved up. Tempo drove across the bridge, with bees trailing from the vehicle. Upon reaching the suspension girders, the van suddenly hit one side of the road and swerved in the middle of the bridge, almost turning all the way around.

A loud *"Ahhh!"* came from the crowd.

"It's the commander, Mr. Big, from the Lord's Liberation Army, thrown from the van!" yelled Jason. Several men started down toward the wreck, but then ran back when they saw the angry bees.

The three occupants of the van crawled away screaming in pain. Tempo, without his handgun, crawled on the bridge. Rufu's hands and arms waved about his head and shoulders.

Munonga was shouting over and over again, "Tempo, watch me. Where in hell are you?"

Lugazi and Jason directed the men to capture the unarmed trio and tie them up with rope.

Jason watched the swarm, a dark mistlike cloud, rise higher and heard a louder buzz. He felt the whipping air as bees swung fast and violent over the crowd. Then the swarm rose still higher on the girder, growing larger and noisier.

Now nobody was brave or foolhardy enough to follow Munonga's attempt to cross the river bridge. However, Lugazi knew how to handle bees. Jason and the tall man, with blankets over their heads and armloads of dry grass, went toward the bridge. After they placed the grass on the girder, the tall man lit it.

The bees were not as ferocious as before, as though they had spent their anger on the men in the blue van. The swarm rose and whirled above the bridge.

Katura said, "I wonder what Grandma will think if we don't come back. We can't cross the bridge and go home."

The tall man inspected and found that most of the bees had gone. "They were waiting for the thief who stole their honey."

"Yes, the bees hoped to get Lugazi. They didn't get to sting him. Instead, they got the bad guys."

Jason and Lugazi turned the sullen Munonga and the protesting Tempo over to the town constable, who would hold them for the national army.

Jason used his cell phone to call Mr. Kamoga, who didn't answer. So he gave Lugazi his phone to call to get someone to pick up the prisoners. Some men from the crowd found the Liberation van midway across the bridge with the keys in it and the motor still running. They drove it up into town with the prisoners tied up inside.

The local constable found Jason and Katura a place to sleep for the night and food. Early the next morning they left for home.

Twenty

THE NEXT MORNING JASON AND Katura walked behind a crowd of people stretching across the highway. They walked down the middle of the road since there was almost no traffic. Taxis had detoured around the bridge.

Jason had just thrown his leg over, getting ready to board the bicycle again, when the loud blast of a horn sounded behind them. It was repeated several times, and people scattered to the sides of the road, stopped, and looked back. Jason and Katura recognized the army jeep, followed by the big transport army carrier. It moved up slowly behind them.

In the jeep's front seat, sitting beside the driver, was Lieutenant Ndugwa waving his short baton. Jason looked closely at the occupants of both vehicles, expecting to see Biraro.

The driver parked smartly beside them, and the lieutenant greeted Jason and Katura with smiles, handshakes, and hugs.

Jason looked over the lieutenant's shoulder while greeting him and, in almost the same breath, asked, "But where's . . . ?"

"Oh, your friend, Biraro? He's already gone to camp for training. We are very short of personnel and have to get more trained people in the field."

Beside him, Katura was disappointed until she saw Selina and her mother in back of the big truck with three captured women. Katura ran back to talk to them. Selina quickly joined her on the ground, laughing and hugging her. Selina and Mrs. Kamoga explained they were accompanying the poachers' women to the camp where they would be sent to Kampala and Nairobi. She explained that the women legally should have a female matron with them when they were imprisoned, and Mr. Kamoga had asked her to accompany them. The three women were sad and unresponsive, bundled in the back of the big truck, whispering to each other. The one called Markia complained, blaming herself for ever leaving Dar es Salaam. They huddled together, wrapping their shawls more tightly, silent.

Lieutenant Ndugwa said to Jason, "Last night after your message was relayed by MP Kamoga, my unit followed your directions to their camp and took these women. The three leading poachers took off in a Land Rover, and Abdul and Bombo escaped in a van, leaving the women. We chased them down to where the tanker crashed, but we got there just after that blast. Those three poachers were in the middle of it. The Australian was burnt badly, but they think he will live. The other two are burned and scarred in a Mubende hospital. They looked horrible, near death. Now they know how the animals feel."

He stopped short. "Mr. Kamoga was very critical of me. He said I should have brought you along after you escaped from the Liberation Army camp. But . . . wait! I'm forgetting something important. Where is your cell? Your grandmother has been trying to call you for two days."

"If it rang, we were somehow too busy or occupied to hear it."

"Well, your grandmother needs you at home right away."

"Why? What's wrong? Is Mbabazi still helping her?"

"I don't want to alarm you, but it sounds serious. Load your bicycle on the truck, and you and your sister come with me in my vehicle. We will drive you there. The truck can deliver them to Kampala, and come back and meet us at your house."

TWENTY-ONE

WHEN LIEUTENANT NDUGWA'S JEEP DROVE into the yard of Jason's house in the canyon near the game park, everything was in disarray. The whole place was turned upside down. First, Jason noticed the tall lampposts with wires stretched on them and lights dangling from their tops. So the game park and government were finally installing lights. He was proud and touched Katura's arm. But then he saw the animals near the fence on the park side. They were gazing, raising their heads often, almost like they were looking for something in Jason's yard.

Several elephants slowly circled around and deer nibbled grasses near the gate, but they were waiting and watching. Even the warthogs raised their snouts instead of rooting. He noticed Necktie, Katura's giraffe, slowly nibbling buds on a nearby mimosa. All of the animals were standing about as if they obeyed some kind of summons. As if they, too, wanted to know what was happening there.

Everything in the yard indicated some disaster had occurred. Beds were moved outside, stripped of bedding, leaning against the walkway. Blankets, sheets, pillowcases, mattresses, and clothing lay drying over the lawn and bushes in the bright sunlight. Something major had happened. His people and many

Africans don't like to sleep in a room where someone has died; they associated death with some evil spirit, and so they cleansed everything in the house right away. A part of him knew . . .

He heard pounding in the front yard. As he got out of the vehicle, Grandma came around waving a stick. She had been throwing soapy water onto a rug and beating it out. She stood there with both arms out and doubled fists shaking. Jason couldn't see her face, but she ran to them with tears in her eyes and grabbed them in a strong hug. She held both children close, spilling her tears on them.

"Come to Grandma, my babies!" She hugged both Katura and Jason again. They hung onto her. Lieutenant Ndugwa stood away at a respectful distance.

"Don't cry! Your grandmother loves you, and I am so sorry I sent you away." It was unlike Grandma to break down. Jason knew she cried not only for herself, but for Katura, Asia, and him. He knew before she said it that their mother was dead.

She repeated, "Please don't cry." But both Jason and Katura asked at the same time.

"Is mother . . . ?" They both gripped her arm and looked into her face. She squeezed both of them. "Gone! Both of them are gone! Mother and father, my children motherless and fatherless! I only have you left in the world."

"I thought it when Lieutenant Ndugwa said you wanted us home. How is my little sister?" said Katura.

"Just fine. Go on in and see her. I'm cleaning everything. Look quickly and come away."

Jason knew Grandma was thinking that although AIDS could only be transmitted by blood and very close contact, she was taking no chances. She observed the tradition to keep away from a place of death.

Then Grandma remembered and went over to greet the lieutenant. "How are you, sir? Thanks for bringing my children home. Come sit in one of these chairs. You are welcome. I am alone. I sent the girl Mbabazi home. She has been such a help, but now she needed to go to her mother."

Katura hurried through the front door and came out holding a cooing Asia. Jason thought Asia had grown much bigger while they were gone. Grandma apologized to the lieutenant for not having tea ready.

"I regret but I must leave soon," he said. Jason must come with him and make a report about the people just captured and give information about the captured poachers and descriptions of the two still at large, Bombo and Abdul.

"Well, he'll be back. He is the man of this family now," said Grandma.

Jason had not had time to think, to consider how his parents' deaths might affect his future. Suddenly he realized that he now had to take care of his two sisters.

"We have already sent your mother to Grandpa at our place, where we will bury her. So all of us will go there. Anyway, you kids can't stay here any longer. They will appoint another ranger who will take over this place."

Then they all heard Grandma's cell phone ringing. She ran inside to answer it. "That must be your Grandpa," she said over her shoulder. A few moments later, she shouted, "Jason, please come in. It's Mbabazi and she has news for you."

He ran in, thinking she must have heard from Biraro.

"I didn't know you had returned. I was just calling to tell Grandma the great news," she said, bubbling with excitement. "Top scores on your O-level examination! Both you and Biraro scored near the top of the class. Mother says it's in all the papers, along with a lot of news about a petrol tanker explosion killing many people."

"Thanks very much. Here, tell Grandma."

She took the phone and gleefully listened to the girl.

Jason went in to wash up and change his grubby clothing. He took clean shirts and pants from his father's closet. Then he crept and looked ever so briefly into the sick room where father and now their mother had died. He and Katura had joined the many youth of Africa and the world that had lost parents to the deadly epidemic.

Katura came to the hallway near him, holding the baby. He held onto both of them in the doorway gazing at the empty space where their mother's bed used to be. The room was empty now. Empty.

He hugged the baby and Katura again for a long time. Then he went to put on his regular shoes, but he knew he would be walking in his father's shoes from now on. Katura followed him with their baby sister.

Jason was both sad and happy. They had passed, and passed with high honors. He and Biraro were assured of scholarships any place they chose to go. But what choice did he have, really? He could not leave his two sisters. He loved them. He needed them and they needed him. He had to take care of them. He had to earn a living for them.

"Both you and Biraro passed high. You must be proud," she said.

He hugged Katura and took the baby in his arms, holding her tenderly near his face, smiling with her, feeling her warm breath on his face.

"They are just exam scores." He decided right then that he would join the army or do anything, do any job to take care of his sisters. Biraro had said outside the Shelsia Clinic that *"Sometimes life makes choices for us."* Now Jason could understand that.

He said goodbye to his sister and his grandmother and sat quietly in the jeep beside Lieutenant Ndugwa. The lieutenant was silent for a while. Then he said, "Mr. Kamoga said last night he was quite sure the oil companies would have to set up research labs near the oil find. He would not give up, and that tanker explosion almost assured his success. The oil company is liable for all of those deaths and destruction of property."

With that announcement, Jason could visualize changes happening all around him. Tomorrow was a new day. There would be a time when things would be different in the country. Useful things could be made right here in Uganda and research would be done locally, with the approval and knowledge of its citizens.

THE END

ABOUT THE AUTHOR

Moses Leon Howard is an American
writer and educator who has been writing for children and adults for fifty
years. A retired dean of a community
college, biology teacher, assistant high
school principal, and counselor/
mentor for students at risk, he lives in
Tacoma, Washington.

Mr. Howard has written four novels, three children's
books, and numerous short stories, and has completed a
historic novel about Nzinga Mbande, a woman who ruled for
forty years in seventeenth century Angola.

In addition to his career as an educator in the U.S., Mr.
Howard served as a Fulbright Fellow in Africa and spent ten
years training medical technologists and preparing secondary
school teachers in Kampala, Uganda.

Learn more, and find more publications by Mr. Howard,
at http://jugumpress.com/MosesHoward/.

ACKNOWLEDGMENTS

My gratitude to my mother, Missoura Bradley Howard, who believed I could write and encouraged me from an early age. To Deborah Cherry, my talented writing partner who was a constant reader and an effective copyeditor along the way.

I am grateful to Ann Scorgie, my copy editor at Heinemann Educational books, who made my first books, *Dogs of Fear* and *The Ostrich Chase*, popular when books about African teens were not often read. Also to Lee Wyndham, writing teacher at New York University, who taught me about heroes and villains in stories for children and teenagers. A special thanks to Miriam Chaikin, former Children's fiction editor at Holt Rinehart and Winston, who heard the music in *The Human Mandolin*. I also thank my children Bonnie, Rodney, Kitita, Ralph, Hodari, Ngoma, Bilori, Morningside, and Ruganzu, who keep reminding me that a future book must be dedicated to their mother.

ABOUT JUGUM PRESS

Jugum Press, a small independent publisher, presents an eclectic collection of fiction, historic monographs, memoirs, and the *Opera en Español* series.

Jugum Press titles are available at online stores, and you can request these books from your local bookseller.

A Boy from Wannaska
by Marjorie W. Mortensen

> Sparkling tales of life in a tiny northern Minnesota town amidst first-generation Scandinavian immigrants in the early twentieth century.

Journey Into Gold Country: Memories of a Forty-Niner
by Ralph Buckingham; foreword by Charles Barker

> Three wild years in the California Gold Rush, remembered in tranquility sixty years later by a New England younger son of a youngest son who went to seek his fortune.

Find print and ebook editions
and sign up to receive notice of new books
by Moses L. Howard and other writers at:
www.jugumpress.com